Hugh Glass, Mountain Man

Robert M. McClung

MORROW JUNIOR BOOKS
NEW YORK

For Gale

ILLUSTRATIONS CREDITS

Permission is gratefully acknowledged: courtesy Department of Library Services, American Museum of Natural History, pp. 83 (Neg. #34567), 85 (Neg. #326443, Photo: Rota); courtesy of The Century Company, reprinted in The Splendid Wayfaring *by John G. Niehardt, Macmillan, 1920, p. 5; Robert M. McClung, pp. viii–ix, 49, 157; National Park Service, p. 80 (drawing by Paul Rockwell); Rare Books and Manuscripts Division, The New York Public Library, Astor, Lenox and Tilden Foundations, pp. 23, 135, 154;* The Royal Natural History, *edited by Richard Lydekker (1893–94), pp. 14 and 123 (engravings by G. Mützel), 34 and 43 (engravings by F. Specht), 100; National Anthropological Archives, Smithsonian Institution, pp. 63, 86, 89; Walters Art Gallery, Baltimore, pp. 64, 70, 73, 118, 150.*

Inquiries should be addressed to
William Morrow and Company, Inc.,
105 Madison Avenue, New York, NY 10016.
Printed in the United States of America.
1 2 3 4 5 6 7 8 9 10
Library of Congress Cataloging-in-Publication Data
McClung, Robert M.
Hugh Glass, mountain man/Robert M. McClung.
p. cm.
Includes bibliographical references. Summary: A fictionalized biography of the legendary hero of the Old West, who as a fur trapper in 1823, survived an attack by a grizzly bear.
ISBN 0-688-08092-8.
1. Glass, Hugh, ca. 1780-ca. 1833—Juvenile fiction. [1. Glass, Hugh, ca. 1780-ca. 1833—Fiction. 2. Survival—Fiction. 3. Frontier and pioneer life—Fiction. 4. West (U.S.)—Fiction.] I. Title.
PZ7.M1337Hu 1990 [Fic]—dc20 90-37814 CIP AC

Contents

Foreword

On March 20, 1822, the following notice appeared in the St. Louis *Missouri Republican*:

> TO ENTERPRISING YOUNG MEN
>
> The subscriber wishes to engage One Hundred Men to ascend the Missouri River to its source, there to be employed for one, two or three years. For particulars enquire of Major Andrew Henry near the lead mines in the county of Washington, who will ascend with, and command the party; or of the subscriber near St. Louis.
>
> (Signed) William H. Ashley

This notice signaled the beginnings of the Rocky Mountain Fur Company, an organization destined to become famous in the annals of the West for the almost legendary explorations and daring deeds carried out by members of the company during the next few years.

That year, Major Henry took the first group of trappers up the Missouri River by keelboat as far as the mouth of the Yellowstone River, near the present boundary between North Dakota and Montana. Here, in a rugged and almost unknown wilderness area rich in beaver streams, he established a trading post he named Fort Henry.

During that winter, the little company of mountain men lost many of their horses to marauding Assiniboine Indians. Worse, four of the trappers were killed by Blackfoot warriors. These native Americans, understandably, did not care for this invasion of their land by white men.

Back in St. Louis, General Ashley ran another newspaper ad in the spring of 1823 to enlist additional recruits for the struggling fur company. Hugh Glass was one of these.

Nearly fifty when he joined Ashley, Hugh was much older than most of the other men. His younger companions often referred to him as Old Glass or Graybeard.

Reserved by nature and somewhat of a loner, Hugh Glass seldom talked about himself. Years after the events of this story, however, he told his friend and fellow mountain man George Yount something of his early history. Before becoming a trapper and mountain man, Hugh related, he had been a mariner. He'd had the ill luck of having his ship captured by the notorious pirate Jean Lafitte, who had been terrorizing the Texas Gulf Coast for many years. Given the choice of either joining the pirates or being killed, he had chosen life. Unable to endure the depraved pirate life for long, he and a companion escaped by jumping overboard one dark night and swimming to the shore two miles away.

Making their way northward from the Texas Coast, the two were eventually captured by a band of Pawnee Indians, and Hugh was forced to watch while his companion was tortured and killed. Then it was Hugh's turn. As the Indians started to tie him to the stake, he nonchalantly pulled from his belt a small bag of vermilion he had brought with him from the pirate ship for trading purposes. Knowing that this bright red warpaint was prized by the Indians, he ceremoniously presented it to the chief. Impressed by this show of courage, the Indian leader saved Hugh from death by adopting him. Hugh lived with the Indians—and as an Indian—for many months. Eventually he accompanied the Pawnee leaders when they traveled to St. Louis on a peace mission. It was there, in the spring of 1823, that he signed on as a trapper with the Rocky Mountain Fur Company.

Full of danger, hardships, and hairbreadth escapes as his life had been up to this point, the series of remarkable adventures that Hugh Glass experienced during the next few months were even more astonishing. Their telling forms the substance of this book.

All the principal events described here are firmly established as history. However, many of the details, as related by various contemporaries of Hugh Glass, differ.This book is written as fiction but is solidly based on the historical accounts. Hugh Glass was a real person who, because of

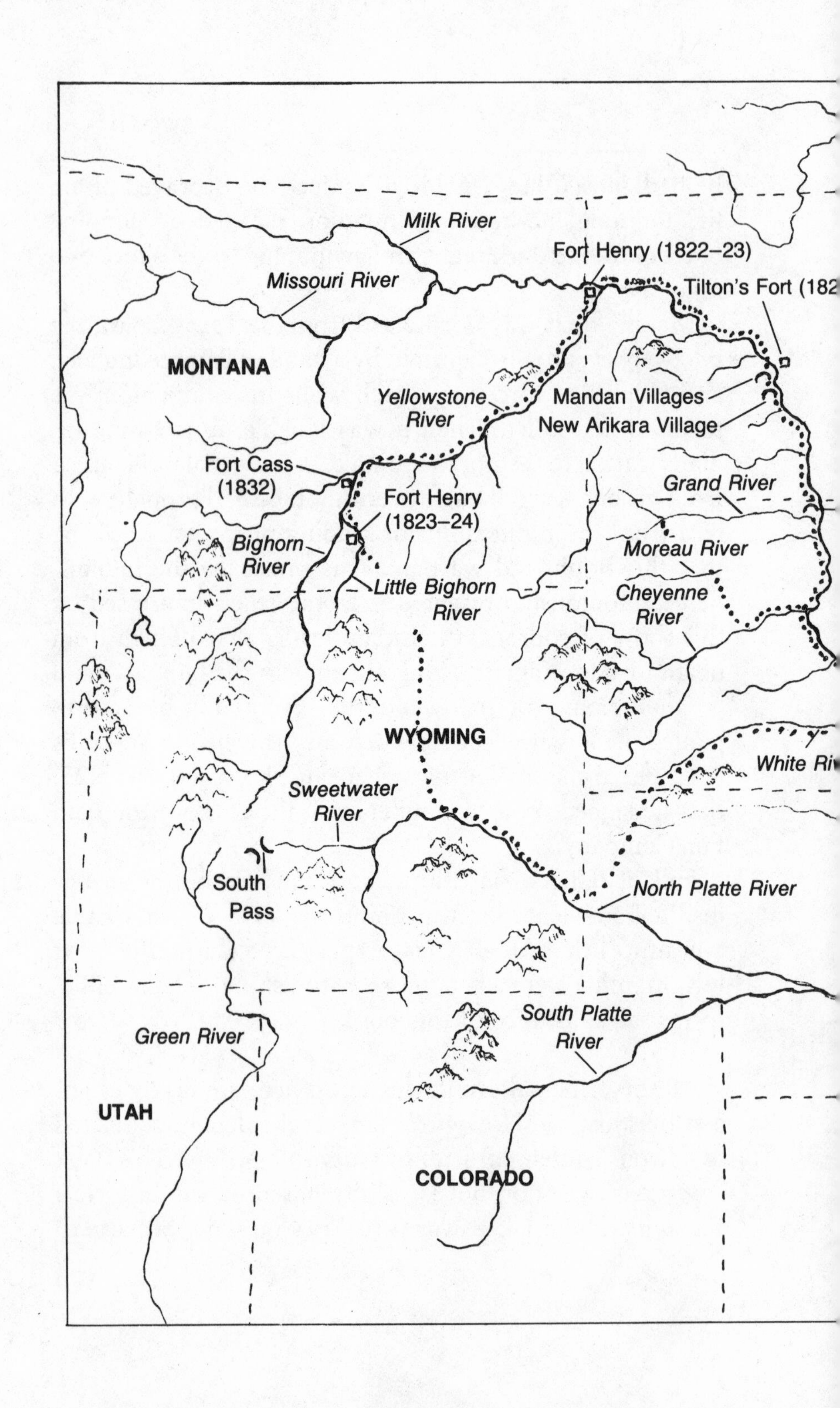
Milk River
Fort Henry (1822–23)
Missouri River
Tilton's Fort (182
MONTANA
Yellowstone River
Mandan Villages
New Arikara Village
Fort Cass (1832)
Grand River
Fort Henry (1823–24)
Bighorn River
Moreau River
Little Bighorn River
Cheyenne River
WYOMING
White Ri
Sweetwater River
South Pass
North Platte River
South Platte River
Green River
UTAH
COLORADO

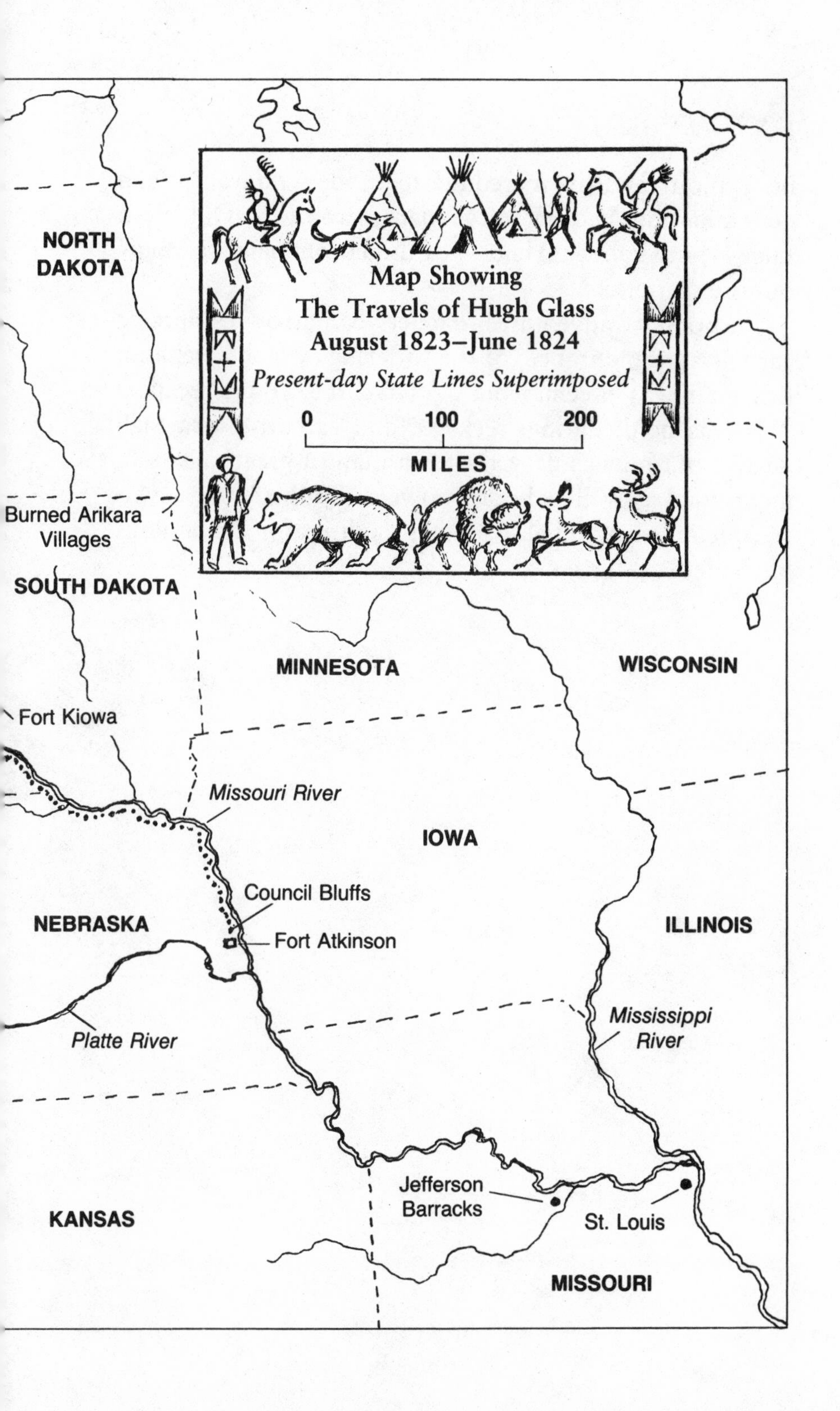
Map Showing
The Travels of Hugh Glass
August 1823–June 1824
Present-day State Lines Superimposed
0
100
200
MILES
NORTH DAKOTA
Burned Arikara Villages
SOUTH DAKOTA
MINNESOTA
WISCONSIN
Fort Kiowa
Missouri River
IOWA
Council Bluffs
NEBRASKA
Fort Atkinson
ILLINOIS
Mississippi River
Platte River
Jefferson Barracks
KANSAS
St. Louis
MISSOURI

his exploits and his incredible fortitude, endurance, and determination, became a legendary hero of the Old West. Luck—both good and bad—featured prominently in many of his experiences.

"In point of adventures, dangers & narrow escapes & capacity for endurance, & the sufferings which befel him, this man was preeminent . . . ," George Yount recalled. "He was bold, daring, reckless, and eccentric to a high degree, but he was nevertheless a man of great talents & intellectual as well as bodily power—But his bravery was conspicuous beyond all his other qualities for the perilous life he led. . . ."

1
Ambush at the Forks of the Grand

A golden eagle floated slowly through the cloudless sky, searching the rolling grasslands beneath it for possible prey. Below and to its right were low bluffs fringed with small cottonwoods and willows, marking the meandering course of the Grand River. Ahead, the waving grass appeared as a golden sea, dotted here and there with the silver blue of sage. Seemingly endless, the high Dakota prairie swept to the horizon in gentle waves, interrupted only to the south by the far-off mass of Thunder Butte, like a distant ship upon the sea.

Almost directly beneath the big feathered hunter, a

group of men and horses were making their way through the scrub growth beside the river. The men were walking, for the few horses they had with them were loaded down with traps and other equipment. The leader of the group looked up, watching as the eagle veered away to hunt in areas undisturbed by the passage of his company.

The date was August 23, 1823. Major Andrew Henry of the Rocky Mountain Fur Company and his party of twelve trappers had started out five days before, heading westward from the junction of the Missouri and Grand Rivers toward Henry's post on the Yellowstone. There they aimed to snug down for the winter and a season of beaver trapping.

It was midafternoon, but the sun was still high in the sky. Calling a brief halt, Major Henry beckoned three of the men to him, and instructed them to push on ahead of the rest of the party to try to get some fresh meat for the evening meal.

"And I don't need to tell you," he added, "keep your eyes peeled for any sign of Indians. We don't want anything like last night to happen again."

Hugh Glass nodded in silent agreement, as did Black Harris and Jim Bridger. Last night a band of Indians—Arikaras most likely—had outwitted the guards and crept up on the camp while everyone else was asleep. They'd killed two men—Jim Anderson and Augie Neill—and then made off before the rest of the trappers had even begun to get untangled from their blankets. A bad business.

A half hour later, Hugh and the other two men had spread out more than a mile ahead of the rest of the party and were searching the prairie land ahead for game. Closest to the river, Hugh Glass marched steadily ahead through the buffalo grass, his keen eyes missing nothing around him. A half mile away to his left was young Jim Bridger, and beyond him was Black Harris. With luck, the company would have some good red meat for the evening meal. A young buffalo cow would taste good tonight, Hugh thought, but venison or antelope steaks would do just as well.

A full six feet tall, Hugh was a rugged figure, lean but broad-shouldered and muscular. His clear eyes were gray-blue, his thick hair and beard black, though heavily streaked with gray. He was dressed in the typical mountain man's outfit—fringed buckskin hunting shirt and breeches, with his feet encased in moccasins. Even though the weather of late summer was still warm, he wore a wolfskin cap. A leather belt, slung over his left shoulder and under his right arm, carried the ammunition for his flintlock rifle. His powder horn and several small leather bags containing flint and steel, pipe tobacco, salt, sugar, and a few other "fixin's" hung from a broad leather girdle around his waist. A hatchet and hunting knife were tucked into the belt as well.

Most of the company's trappers were young men, Hugh reflected, with nineteen-year-old Jim Bridger the youngest of them all. And he was the oldest. Let the others call him Graybeard, he told himself with a slight smile. He could still hold his own with any of them, even though he was almost fifty years old and had a gimpy leg at the moment.

Hugh walked with a slight limp, the result of a leg wound he had received in a fight with the Arikara Indians a couple of months earlier. Most of the Rocky Mountain Fur Company's horses had been killed during that encounter. That was why everyone in the present party was heading for the Yellowstone on foot instead of riding.

A grizzled ball of gray tumbleweed rolled past Hugh as he tramped on, and a red-tailed hawk wheeled lazily in the blue sky above him. A squat badger, interrupted in its task of digging after gophers, snarled disagreeably as it scurried into the brush beside the river. Hugh saw all of these, but paid them no further attention. His eyes were continually sweeping the grasslands ahead for deer or pronghorn antelope, or even a band of buffalo.

At the same time, he was alert, as always, for Indian signs. This was risky territory here at the forks of the Grand, with the Arikaras—the mountain men called them "Rees"—on the warpath. They would be like angry hornets, Hugh told himself, buzzing about and itching to lift the scalps of any whites they might encounter. Yes sirree! Those Rees would be out for vengeance, after the burning of their villages just two weeks ago.

Hugh shook his head as he thought back over all that had happened since last March, when he and the other new recruits had joined the Rocky Mountain Fur Company after they'd seen that newspaper notice. Led by General Ashley, they had set out from St. Louis in two keelboats with high hopes, aiming to join up with Major Henry and the old hands on the Yellowstone. Progress had been slow, for they'd had to buck high waters and strong currents. Time and again, floating trees had swept downriver, threatening to crash into the boats and swamp them.

June had come before they reached the junction of the Grand River with the Missouri in Dakota territory. Here

Cordelling a keelboat. When the crew is unable to make headway by sailing or poling, some of them disembark and pull the boat upstream by long towlines.

they'd stopped near two villages of Arikara Indians, to trade with them for horses needed at the Yellowstone post. The Rees had seemed friendly enough, but before dawn one morning they had launched a surprise attack, killing thirteen of the Rocky Mountain Fur Company men and wounding eleven others, including Hugh. Remembering that fight, Hugh rubbed his right thigh, where the ball had gone in, and grimaced. That leg still gave him a bit of trouble, especially after a long day's tramp.

After that battle with the Rees, the trappers retreated downriver to the mouth of the Cheyenne, and General Ashley sent a messenger, Jedediah Smith, overland to Fort Henry, asking for reinforcements. Responding quickly, Major Henry and a group of the old hands joined them several weeks later. In late July, a company of soldiers under Colonel Leavenworth traveled upriver from Fort Atkinson and joined them too. So did a brigade of Missouri Fur Company trappers and several hundred friendly Sioux Indians—Dakotas.

The combined forces marched back upriver and, in early August, laid siege to the Arikara villages and pounded them with artillery. Outnumbered and outgunned, the Rees quickly asked for a truce, which Colonel Leavenworth granted. The next night, under cover of darkness, the Rees abandoned their villages and escaped undetected into the wilderness. Disgusted, some of the Missouri Fur Company men set fire to the deserted villages the next morning. They'd have liked to wipe out the Rees once and for all.

After the campaign, the Rocky Mountain Fur Company men had gone their separate ways. General Ashley returned to St. Louis with a few of the men, while some of the others headed upriver in the keelboat *Rocky Mountains* with supplies for Fort Henry. A third group, under Jedediah Smith, headed westward to explore the regions beyond the Black Hills. The fourth party, under Major Henry, was making its way overland through the Grand River valley to the Yellowstone.

Hugh was one of this group. And here he was today, looking for game for the evening meal.

As he walked around a thick clump of tumbleweed, he glimpsed a slight movement in a stand of bushes near the river. Before he could react, four prongbucks bounded into view a hundred yards away, and headed for the open prairie. Raising his flintlock as quickly as he could, Hugh fired at the last antelope—but too late. Unhurt, it dashed away, its white rump bouncing up and down.

Exasperated, Hugh stared after the antelope. He should have had that one! All four of the pronghorns, he noted, were bounding toward the area where Jim Bridger and Black Harris were hunting. Maybe they'd have better luck. In the meantime, he'd reload Old Faithful and be ready if another chance came his way.

Holding the flintlock by the barrel, Hugh carefully poured powder from his horn into the muzzle, then popped a ball into the barrel and rammed the charge home. Old Faithful was ready once again for whatever came along.

He heard the report of a rifle, faint in the distance, then a second shot. Ah, good! That would be Bridger and Harris shooting. He hoped they'd gotten at least one of the antelope. It was about time to make camp for the night, and he for one was mighty hungry.

Just ahead and to his left was a thicket of wild plums and chokecherries fringing a small creek that fed into the Grand. Eyeing the trees loaded with dark red fruit, he headed toward them. He would eat a few plums and wet his whistle. That would tide him over for a bit.

Stripping a handful of the plump fruit from the nearest branch, he swallowed the juicy flesh and spit out the pits. As he reached out to pick a few more, he heard a faint splash from the creek. Instantly alert, he stopped and peered in that direction. A thicket of trees and bushes blocked his view.

He heard the splash a second time. More prongbucks? Buffalo? Indians? Advancing cautiously toward the water, he parted the thick foliage ahead of him, trying to determine what had made the noise.

A surprised snort exploded from the creek bed, then a

grunting exhalation of breath. Looming up in front of him, less than thirty feet away, was a huge grizzly bear. Old Ephraim, or white bear, was what trappers called the beast. This one was a female. She was rooting in the stream bank, and her jaws dripped with roots and bulblets. Her squinty eyes were peering straight in Hugh's direction.

He froze in his tracks, his muscles tensed. The bear was too close for him to get away if she charged. The question was—had she seen him? Hugh could see the silvered cinnamon hairs on her shoulders rising, as though in answer to possible danger.

Rearing onto her hind legs, the big bear sniffed loudly, her leathery snout wiggling back and forth as she tested the air. In the shallow stream bed behind her, Hugh glimpsed two good-sized yearling cubs. Each of them, he figured, weighed close to a hundred fifty pounds.

The old grizzly gave a startled whoof as she finally spotted Hugh. Grunting, she dropped to all fours and charged straight at the mountain man. In seconds she was within a few feet of him. Quickly rising once again to her hind legs, the big bear loomed over Hugh like a giant, shaggy boxer. She opened her mouth, lips drawn back to show the great yellowed fangs and grinding teeth, the glistening red tongue and gums. She snarled viciously as she raised her right forepaw, aiming a deadly blow at the man before her.

Hugh had time only to raise his flintlock, aim at her chest, and pull the trigger before the sledgehammer force of the big grizzly's paw knocked him sprawling to the ground. His only thought as he was swept down by the force of that terrible forepaw was that his aim had been true. But the shot hadn't stopped her. He felt the giant bear on top of him, felt the teeth biting into his neck. Ah-h-h—in a minute he'd be dead.

In desperation he pulled out his hunting knife and thrust it into the vast furry bulk above him. Again and again. Growling in pain and anger, the bear seized Hugh's head in her jaws. Blood streamed down over his face and he felt a loose flap of skin hanging over his eyes, blinding him. Screaming, he wrenched free of the grizzly and turned over on his stomach. A moment later he felt the giant's four-inch claws raking his shoulders and backside, cutting his flesh to the bone.

He heard faint shouts in the distance. Someone was coming to help him. Too late, he thought, too late. But he'd fight to the end.

Gritting his teeth, Hugh twisted over on his side and stabbed his knife into the soft underbelly of the enraged grizzly one more time. Then another. The big bear was streaming with blood, as he was, but the knife wounds did not seem to affect her. She growled savagely, and her teeth crunched into his right leg, tearing the skin and the muscle. Hugh could feel her fangs grating on his leg bone, could feel his flesh being torn to ribbons.

Finally the grizzly seized him by the shoulder and shook him violently, much as a dog might shake a rabbit. Hugh felt clouds of blackness coming over him. He stabbed at the bear one last time, then fell back, unconscious.

2
Major Henry's Decision

Jim Bridger, a quarter of a mile away, heard the report of Hugh's rifle, then the growls of the enraged grizzly mixed with Hugh's screams. He started running toward the creek as fast as he could go, at the same time shouting to Black Harris to join him.

The first thing he saw as he approached the creek were the two yearling cubs. Stimulated by their mother's fury, they charged the young mountain man as soon as they spotted him. Jim fired at the leading cub, dropping it. The second kept coming, however, snarling its defiance. Without time to reload his rifle, Bridger retreated into the stream. The cub followed. Black Harris hastened up just in time to kill it with a well-placed shot.

Alerted by the rifle fire and the roars of the bear, the main party had come into sight by this time. Together with Black Harris and Jim Bridger, the trappers approached the spot where the female grizzly lay, her huge body almost hiding that of the man beneath her.

The bear lay with one giant forepaw over Hugh, her long claws still raking his chest, as if protecting her kill. Both man and beast were smeared with blood that streamed from many wounds. Both appeared dead.

His rifle at the ready, Major Henry advanced in front of the others. He threw a small stone at the bear, hitting her on the flank. No response. Satisfied that she was indeed dead, he beckoned the others forward, and they pulled the shaggy beast off the body of their companion. A big bear, the major thought, weighing close to eight hundred pounds. The grizzly's chest was punctured with many knife wounds, as well as the hole made by Hugh's single rifle shot. Turning his attention to Hugh Glass, Major Henry shook his head sadly as he gazed at the mangled body.

"Well, Hugh certainly put up a great battle, killing this old grizzly," he observed, "but she did him in, too."

The other mountain men looked down on the body of their comrade. All of them saw what they thought was a mutilated corpse. Their eyes hardened. There but for the luck of the draw was one of them.

Hugh was sprawled on his back, one leg bent grotesquely under him, the other straight out. Blood oozed from his scalp, and bare bone showed through the torn muscle of his mangled left shoulder. The canine teeth of the white bear had seemingly made mincemeat of his neck and throat. Drops of blood were still bubbling out through the torn skin.

Turning Hugh over, Major Henry saw that his buckskin jacket and breeches were torn and bloody where the lethal claws had ripped into his back and rump. The others stared, sobered yet fascinated by the damage the bear had done.

"Poor Old Glass," Black Harris muttered at last. "He always were a good'n in a fight—'specially when the goin' got thick. But this b'ar was just too much for 'im. Should we bury him right here, Major?"

As if in response, Hugh's eyes suddenly fluttered open. A faint moan issued from the mangled throat. A bloody hand rose several inches, as the moan was repeated. Then the hand dropped and the eyes closed.

"He ain't dead!" Jim Bridger exclaimed in an awed voice. "Leastways, he weren't dead a second ago!"

Major Henry knelt beside the still figure and put his ear next to the chest, listening. He could hear a heartbeat, very faint and ragged.

"He's alive," he agreed, "but from the looks of it, not for long." Glancing at Hugh's face, he saw that the eyes of the wounded man had opened once again, and the pupils were following his movements. The throat quivered and a gurgle came forth. All the men could hear was a choking gasp.

"He's tryin' to say somethin'," Black Harris observed.

"But he can't talk," one of the others said in a low voice. "That b'ar tore a hole in his throat big enough to drive yer fist through!"

Major Henry looked down at the mauled man and

scratched his forehead. Hugh was too far gone to be moved, he reckoned. And with those injuries, he couldn't survive for long; he'd probably be dead by morning.

Henry surveyed the little clearing they were in. It was green with buffalo grass, fringed about the edges with wild plum and chokecherry bushes. And the creek was close by. He glanced at the sky, where the sun was already sinking toward the western horizon. "We'll stop here for the night," he declared. "Harris and I will see what we can do for Old Hugh while the rest of you make camp."

Everyone got to work immediately. Major Henry and Black Harris eased a blanket under Hugh's body, then removed his torn and bloody clothing and washed his wounds in cold water. Although Hugh was barely breathing and the two men considered him as good as dead, they felt obliged, nevertheless, to try to patch him up.

After dousing each raw wound with brandy, Major Henry carefully put the torn flaps of skin on Hugh's neck and scalp back in place. Assisted by Black Harris, he stitched the flaps together with prongbuck sinews. He then did the same with the ragged edges of skin and flesh that had been ripped to the bone on Hugh's leg, shoulder, and back.

"Lucky he can't feel it," he remarked as he finished. "That's about the best I can do."

"You done real well, Major," Harris assured him as they eased their injured comrade back into his tattered jacket and breeches. "But probably all fer nothin'. I figger he'll be dead afore mornin'." He looked down at Hugh and shook his head. "And may the old man die in peace. He were a good'n."

While they were looking after Hugh, the other men were

Pronghorns. America's swiftest mammals, pronghorn antelopes roamed the plains and prairies by the millions in early days. During a trip up the Missouri River in 1843, the noted bird artist John James Audubon saw many of them. Marveling at their swiftness, he noted that ". . . they fleet by the hunter like flashes or meteors."

busy, too, each doing his assigned task. Acting as cook, Hiram Allen set about building a fire for the evening meal. Jim Bridger had retrieved the pronghorn antelope that Black Harris had shot, skinned it, and cut off choice portions of meat for the evening meal. Four of the other men skinned the two bear cubs, then looped a section of rope around each of the carcasses, as well as that of the old grizzly. Three horses were brought up to drag the bodies of the bears some distance out onto the open prairie. The wolves and vultures would make short work of them there, and the men wouldn't be bothered in the camp. Finally, the horses were watered, then picketed to graze.

It was dusk by the time the mountain men finished their meal. As they smoked a last pipe before turning in, the major posted two men for the first watch and designated those who were to relieve them in succession every two hours throughout the night. It was vitally important to have alert men on watch all night long, what with vengeful Rees scattered all over the country.

As darkness fell, the trappers wrapped themselves in their blankets and slept, all except Black Harris and Hiram Allen, who were taking the first watch. After them, the successive sentinels stood guard throughout the night, their rifles loaded and ready, their eyes peering into the darkness for any suspicious movement, their ears ready to pick up any suspicious sound. At the end of each shift, the guards would check Hugh, lying bandaged and unconscious on a blanket near the embers of the fire. It was too dark to see much, however. All they could hear was an occasional raspy breath from the wounded man.

Major Henry himself took the crucial predawn guard duty, from two to four in the morning. Those were the hours when a surprise attack was most likely. As his partner, he'd selected Jim Bridger. The youngest of the company, Jim had better ears and eyes than most, and had proved himself during the past winter on the Yellowstone. They'd had Indian problems there, too.

The moon had set and, as usual, the hours before dawn were the darkest. The two men heard wolves snarling and scuffling far out on the prairie, as they gorged on the remains of the grizzly bears. Then Bridger heard the quavering hoot of an owl from the thicket by the stream. When he heard it, he tensed and waited, listening with bated breath. Indians sometimes imitated an owl's call when signaling one another. Finally he saw a dark shape—a big bird—rise from the trees and fly silently overhead. He signed with relief. Only an owl, after all.

At dawn, Major Henry went to check Hugh Glass, expecting to find him dead. No sound had come from him during the last watch, and he lay as he had the evening before. Kneeling, the major stared intently at Hugh, then laid an ear to his chest. Was he dead? Finally the major detected a faint heartbeat and saw the eyelids flutter. Hugh was still alive—but just barely. He looked at the bloodstained man and shook his head in disbelief. Glass was obviously near death; what kept him hanging on?

While Major Henry stared at Hugh, Jim Bridger came up and knelt beside the wounded man. He examined him for a long moment, then began to swab gently at Hugh's face with a damp cloth, trying to wipe away some of the dried blood. Hugh moaned. Young Jim then dribbled a few drops of water into Hugh's mouth from a tin cup. Blood bubbled from the mangled throat, and the lips moved, as if trying to say something. No sound came out—just a whistle of breath. Then the eyes closed and Glass slumped once again into unconsciousness.

"It ain't much use, son," Major Henry said to Jim. "I'm afraid he's a goner. That grizzly has done him in. But thanks for trying."

After breakfast, Major Henry called a council of all the men. "We've got to get going to the Yellowstone," he told them. "Old Hugh is so far gone we can't take him with us," he added, then paused for a moment. "But we can't just leave him here, either."

He peered about the group of silent, waiting men. They nodded in silent agreement. You don't just abandon a wounded comrade, even if he's on his deathbed. On the other hand, if they camped here in hostile Indian country till he did die, the rest of them might go under, too.

Major Henry looked at his men once again, his dark blue eyes searching the face of each man in turn. "I'm calling for volunteers," he said finally. "Volunteers who'll stay with Old Hugh till he dies, then bury him proper and catch up with the rest of us."

The men shifted uncomfortably, looking sideways at one another or at the ground. No one spoke up.

"It won't be long," the major said. "He's bound to go most any time. And Old Glass would be the first to forgive the rest of us for not tarrying here. He'd know better'n most that we've got to get to the Yellowstone as fast as we can. How about it?" he asked again. "Who'll stay to see him properly buried?"

Again the men stirred uneasily. Hugh had been a good old hoss—helped more than one of them during the past several months.

Jim Bridger thought back to the battle with the Arikaras, hardly more than ten days ago. He'd advanced toward the Indian villages beside Hugh, and when the Indians began shooting at them from the palisades, the older man had steadied him when he got excited and had pulled him down to safety when the bullets started whistling overhead. Suddenly Jim made up his mind.

"Major, I'll stay with him," he blurted out. "He were good to me."

Major Henry nodded gravely, approving the boy's spirit. Jim was still a lad, not even in his twenties yet. He'd signed on as a greenhorn, fresh from the farm and the blacksmith shop where he'd been apprenticed after the death of his parents. Even so, he'd proved his worth as a hunter, trapper, and Indian fighter with the best of his companions during the past year.

"Well spoken, Jim," Major Henry said warmly. "But we need another volunteer to stay, too." He looked around again at the circle of mountain men.

Finally John Fitzgerald spoke up. He was one of those recruits who had signed up a year ago, as Jim Bridger had. About twenty-five years old, John was quiet and a bit standoffish, but nobody could fault anything he'd done since he'd joined the company.

"You're askin' a lot, Major," he declared. "I'm as unhappy about poor Old Glass as anyone," he continued, "but whoever stays here with Glass risks losin' his hair, like as not. It might set better if you'd make it worth a man's while to stay on. Mebbe the company'd give a man a bonus, say, fer riskin' his scalp and stayin' here."

"Fair enough," Major Henry declared, with a shrug of his shoulders. "Young Jim has already said he'd stay, so I'll give him and any other man that says the same a forty-dollar bonus."

"In that case," Fitzgerald said, "I'll stay behind with Bridger. We'll look after Old Hugh till he dies. Then we'll bury him and ketch up with you at the Yellowstone."

"Good enough," replied Major Henry. "And as you're

older than Jim, I'm putting you in charge. But young Jim has already had a season on the Yellowstone, like you. I know that the two of you will share the responsibilities, like and like."

The matter decided, the major ordered camp to be broken. Within an hour the main party was on its way, heading westward across the prairies.

As he watched them disappear, Jim suddenly felt lonely, even with Fitzgerald there beside him and Hugh Glass lying limp and bloody on the blanket by the remains of the fire.

"We gotta keep a good lookout all the time," Fitz observed. "This is one dangerous country right now. Let's hope the old man passes on real quick. Then we kin ketch up with the lads afore another day—each forty dollars richer t'boot."

Jim looked at him half scornfully, then shivered as his gaze shifted to their wounded companion.

3
The Vigil

"Poor old hoss," Jim murmured as he looked at the torn and bloody figure on the blanket. What could they do, he wondered, to make Hugh's last hours easier?

Heading for a nearby spring that emptied into the creek, he filled a small kettle with cold water and brought it back. He then tore a strip from an old shirt. Wetting it, he began once again to wipe the dried blood away from his wounded companion's face and neck.

Hugh's eyes fluttered open and his lips moved. A faint gurgle came from the torn throat. He's trying to tell me something, Jim thought, but he can't talk. After a moment,

Hugh's eyes closed again. Jim felt his forehead. Hot and feverish. The old man gave a feeble moan.

John Fitzgerald, who had been sitting by the fire, came over to look at their patient. "He won't last the day," he muttered. "And the sooner he dies the better—both fer him and fer us."

The youth did not reply. He continued to clean the dried blood from Hugh's wounds, then checked the bandages and poured cold water over them. The cold-water treatment was the common remedy for any ailments in the wilderness, when no medicines were available. Many a mountain man swore by it to cure wounds or fevers or whatever else might ail a body.

After watching for a while, Fitz got a tin cup of water from the spring and tried to dribble some of it between Hugh's lips. The gray-blue eyes opened for a moment and the cracked lips moved as Hugh tried to swallow a few drops. Most of the water trickled down his chin and onto his gray-streaked beard. Fitz then tried to give him a bit of warm broth left over from the antelope meat they had breakfasted on. Again, most of it ran down Hugh's chin.

"'Tain't no use," Fitzgerald said. "He can't eat, can't talk, and seems like he's burnin' up with fever. He's gonna die."

All that day he and Jim took turns sitting beside the wounded man, changing the strips of cold wet cloth on his forehead and pouring water on the bandaged wounds. They tried repeatedly to get some broth into him, but with little success. Hugh seemed to drift between unconsciousness and awareness. When he was awake, his feverish eyes followed their movements, as if imploring them to do something—anything. Nothing but a few unintelligible croaks came out of the mangled throat. That night the two men alternated standing guard—one watching for possible danger while the other snatched several hours of sleep.

Morning came and Hugh was still breathing, but barely—and the second day passed as the first. Hugh's face was flushed with a high fever. Some of his many wounds had evidently become infected. Jim and Fitz agreed that he couldn't last much longer. That afternoon they dug a shallow grave in the sandy soil under a cottonwood tree. They also collected a pile of rocks to put over the grave when it was filled—to keep the wolves away. Once the end came, they'd be ready to bury Hugh and move on quickly. The second night passed.

The third dawn came and Glass still clung to a thread of life. Fitzgerald, who went out at dawn and dusk each day to check for Indian signs, was increasingly nervous over their situation. That evening he stared at Hugh, as if blaming him for not dying when he was supposed to.

"C'mon, old man," he said, "get it over with." Hugh's eyes suddenly opened, and the wounded man stared at him, as though he had heard and understood.

Fitz felt a flush spread over his face, felt ashamed by Hugh's silent stare. Well, he and Jim were doing their best for him, he reminded himself, but every day that went by increased the danger to themselves.

On the fourth morning of the vigil, Hugh seemed to be sinking. Jim wasn't sure whether he could detect any heartbeat or breathing. The fever had gone and the grizzled face was pale and cool, almost as cold as death. It'll probably be over today, Jim thought.

Herd of bison and elk on the Upper Missouri River. Engraving made from a painting by Karl Bodmer for Travels in the Interior of North America *(1832–34) by Maximilian Alexander Philipp, Prinz von Wied-Neuwied.*

After a cold breakfast, Fitz went out, as usual, to check the area around camp. Keeping close to the brush cover beside the stream, he headed toward the Grand, his eyes sweeping the prairie ahead of him as well as the ground underfoot for any sign of Indians. He'd gone little more than a quarter mile from camp when he discovered what he had dreaded finding in the damp sand beside the creek: fresh pony tracks, the imprints of many moccasins, drag marks where a pony sledge—a travois—had passed. Beside the trail lay a tattered eagle feather with a strip of red flannel tied to its tip.

Fitz drew a sharp breath as he viewed the prints and felt his heart thumping wildly against his rib cage. A dozen or more Indians had gone by—Arikara, no doubt. And these were fresh tracks, no more than a few hours old. They hadn't been here when he came this way last evening. The Indians must have passed at dawn.

Fitz shuddered as visions flashed through his mind of what would've happened if the Indians had stumbled upon Jim and him—and Hugh. Hugh would have been the lucky one. He, at least, was unconscious—beyond caring.

After satisfying himself that the Indians had traveled southward across the open prairie, he hurried back to camp and told Jim what he had found.

"If those Rees had spotted us, it would've been curtains," he assured the younger man. "We gotta get out of here pronto. No use both of us dyin' as well as Old Glass."

Jim did not answer.

"You know what the Rees'll do if they ketch us?" Fitz continued. "They'll lift our scalps and cut us into little pieces!"

"But we can't just leave Hugh," Jim responded. "Not while he's still alive."

"Like hell we can't," Fitz retorted. "I don't aim to die along with the old man if I can help it. Major Henry left me in charge, remember. You'll take your orders from me. And I say we'll be on our way at first light tomorrow mornin'. He'll be dead by then, anyway."

Darkness fell, and the two men sat up watching and waiting, both too worried to sleep. Fitz thought mostly about Indian danger, while Jim pondered the problem of looking out for Hugh Glass. A coyote wailed on a distant butte; then, far off, they heard wolves howling.

At dawn, death had not yet claimed Hugh Glass. Jim

and Fitz both thought he was gone when they first examined him in the faint morning light. Hugh was as pale and still as a corpse, and his skin felt clammy. But when Jim knelt and put an ear to his chest, he detected a whisper of a heartbeat.

"He's good as dead," Fitz exclaimed impatiently, "and we're not doin' him any good by stayin' here with him. I say we should go—right now."

"We can't do that," Jim retorted stubbornly. "We said we'd stay till he died, and I aim to do that. You go on iffen you must, but I'm stayin', at least one more day. He's certain to go under by nightfall."

Fitz flushed angrily. "Major Henry put me in charge," he reminded Jim, "and you'll do as I say." He glared at the youth as he sat down. He couldn't light out without Bridger, he reflected sourly. What would he tell Major Henry and the others?

The hours went by, and more than once Fitz checked to determine whether Hugh had breathed his last. Late that afternoon, he discovered another set of pony tracks on the other side of the camp and returned, even more agitated and fearful than before. Stomping over to Hugh, he peered down at him for a moment, then declared that he was dead. At least he couldn't detect any sign of life.

Jim came over and checked him again, then shook his head. "His heart's still beatin'," he declared. "Ever so faint, though."

Fitzgerald then began to work afresh on the younger man, describing the terrible things the Rees would do if they caught them. "They won't kill us nice and easy," he said. "Oh no." He went on to describe tortures he'd heard about. "Them Rees hate us," he declared, " 'specially since we burned their villages. Any mountain man they ketch they'll kill nice and slow. First they'll scalp 'im alive, then burn 'im at the stake."

Young Jim looked out across the empty prairie, and an image flashed through his mind: a horde of painted warriors on horseback thundering toward him, waving carbines and lances, shooting at him, killing, scalping. . . . He shut his eyes. He didn't want to die any more than Fitz did! His life had just started, he thought to himself, and he still had a heap of living to do.

Thinking about it, he had to admit that a lot of what Fitz was saying was true. They were risking everything by staying here, and Hugh was almost dead, anyway. What difference did it make? He and Fitz had volunteered of their own free will to stay with Hugh, right enough. But Hugh wouldn't want them to die on his account.

He lay awake most of that night, watching, thinking, arguing with himself, fearing that he might hear the war whoops of a band of Rees at any moment.

Fitz was up before dawn, scouting the valley ahead. "C'mon," he ordered as soon as he returned. "We're leavin' right now! The old man's gonna die any minute, anyway." He began to assemble his own gear in his pack. Then he picked up Hugh's rifle and powder horn, his hunting knife, molded shot, and flint and steel.

"You ain't takin' his rifle and all his fixin's, are you?" Jim demanded.

"Sure am," Fitzgerald replied. "He ain't got no use fer 'em where he's goin'. And out in this country you don't leave a dead man's fixin's with him. Major Henry will expect us to bring 'em back when we tell him Old Hugh died and we buried him nice and proper."

He waved his rifle at Jim. "C'mon, boy, let's go!" he ordered. There was ugly menace in his tone.

Jim knelt beside Hugh and saw that he was still breathing, ever so lightly. As he knelt, Hugh's eyes opened briefly, and Jim heard a faint gasp, as if the old man wanted to say something. Then his eyes closed and he lay pale and still.

Jim looked down at the battered and torn body. "Sorry, old hoss," he whispered, "but I know you wouldn't want us to go under, too. There's nothin' more we can do fer ye."

He rose, picked up his gear, and followed Fitzgerald. The two of them had stayed with Hugh for five days and done their best for him, he told himself. Now, maybe Fitz was right. It was time for them to save their own skins and head for the Yellowstone.

4
Abandoned

How long he lay in his deathlike state, Hugh Glass would never know. But eventually it passed, and once again a raging fever returned to wrack his body. He groaned as he felt the heat burning his flesh. His blood seemed to be boiling. Before he'd felt nothing. Now he hurt all over.

His eyes fluttered open. Directly overhead was the sun—a fiery ball searing his flesh. He tried to lift a hand to shield his eyes, but he couldn't. He tried to groan again, but only a stifled gasp came out. Dimly he remembered someone standing over him, looking down. "He's a goner," the figure was saying. "That grizzly has done him in."

The bear! His eyes blinked wide open once again as he saw in his mind's eye the terrible mountain of silver-tipped fur looming over him, jaws open, huge forepaws reaching for him, knocking him to the ground, tearing at his face and head, his neck and throat. Something like a sob burst from his ravaged throat as he tried to escape. Then he sank once more into unconsciousness.

He dreamed. Or was he dreaming? The boy—young Jim—kneeling beside him, placing cold dressings on his wounds, trying to dribble a bit of warm soup into his mouth. The other man—was it Fitz?—saying, "C'mon, we're leavin'. The old man's gonna die any minute, anyway." And young Jim shaking his head.

Hugh woke up and blinked. Where were those two now? Where, for that matter, were Major Henry and the rest of them? Hot hammers seemed to be hitting his head. His eyelids fluttered, then closed. Once again he drifted into unconsciousness. He dreamed.

Scenes flooded his mind as he alternately burned and shivered. Tossing restlessly in his delirium, his raw back scraped against a rock. A sharp searing flash of pain swept through his body like the lash of a cat-o'-nine-tails. He gasped, his eyes opening. A vision of the past appeared before him. Pittsburgh, 1795. It was in Pittsburgh that he'd seen a black slave publicly flogged with a cat-o'-nine-tails for some trifling offense until he'd fallen unconscious. He'd loathed the sight.

He was a gangly nineteen-year-old then, apprenticed to gunsmith Henry Wolfson. And later, when Wolfson had threatened Hugh with a whip for not finishing a walnut rifle stock to his liking, Hugh had wrested the whip from his hand and knocked the gunsmith to the floor. Gunsmith

Wolfson shouldn't have raised his hand to him like that! Picking up the old flintlock willed to him by his father, Hugh had taken off, shipped out on a keelboat heading down the Ohio. Ahead, the western lands. . .

The dreams were jumbled, skipping around through time and space. His little coastal vessel captured by pirates off the Texas Coast. That bloody old cutthroat, Jean Lafitte, giving Hugh and the first mate, Luke, the choice of either joining up with him and his gang of outlaws or walking the plank. They'd already killed the others of his crew. He and Luke had opted for life that time, but they'd waited for their chance to get away. They couldn't abide the heartless cruelty of the pirate gang—murdering the crews of captured vessels, plundering the ships, forcing themselves on any women aboard and then cutting their throats and setting fire to the captured vessels. It didn't bear thinking about. He and Luke had vowed to escape the first chance they got.

One day Lafitte got suspicious of them. He recognized their feelings about pirate life. Then he'd condemned them to death, laughing in their faces as he flung that promise at them. They'd walk the plank the next day, he declared, their hands tied behind their backs, the water below full of sharks.

But Hugh and Luke had outsmarted him. They'd gone overboard in dead of night and swum two miles through the waters of Galveston Bay, wading ashore in a thicket of Texas canebrakes. They'd been lucky that night—the sharks must've been napping! Hugh felt a wild chuckle rising in his torn throat.

He woke with a start, felt the salty sweat on his face

and arms, an agony on the bare wounds. He shivered uncontrollably. Chills, sweats, fever—he had them all. Where was Jim now? He needed that boy to pour cold water on those compresses. He remembered . . . he remembered that long ago time when he'd done the same for his mother and father, and for Rachel and little Ralph, too.

The big woods of western Pennsylvania, his father felling the tall trees with his ax, making a clearing for a cabin. The land was his by rights as a veteran of the Continental Army—bounty land. Hugh was just fifteen then, but already an old hand at hunting and helping his father. His mother tended the cabin and looked after the young ones—Rachel, his blond, ten-year-old sister, and Ralph, his six-year-old baby brother. The black fever struck down the lot of them that second summer. Waugh! He remembered. All of his dear ones were in the ground before fall had come.

Unable to endure the memory, his wandering mind shifted scenes once again. Back to Texas, back to him and Luke. He saw them wading through the canebrake off Galveston . . . scrambling ashore and starting the long walk north. Get as far away from Lafitte and his crew as quickly as possible, they figured, then head for some American settlement in northern Texas. On they wandered, living off the barren land—berries, roots, whatever they could get. On into Kansas—the country of the Pawnees.

Their capture by a war party . . . Hugh forced to stand and watch as the braves danced around Luke tied to a stake, thrusting slivers of burning cedar splints into his flesh. Luke's screams of agony as the flames swept up and over him. Hugh was next . . . and the old feelings flashed through his tortured mind as vivid as when he'd first lived them—steeling himself for the coming torture and death, resolving to meet his end as bravely as possible.

When the Indians turned to seize him, he'd thrust his hand into his hunting shirt and taken out a bag of vermilion he'd brought with him from the pirate ship. Knowing that the Indians prized that blood-red pigment more than nearly anything else, he'd turned to the chief.

"Guess I won't have any use fer this anymore," he heard himself saying to the Pawnee leader. "Here, take it and be damned to ye!"

He remembered the surprised look on the old warrior's face. Chief Black Elk was so astonished by the gift, so impressed with Hugh's bravery and calm acceptance of what was coming, that he adopted him on the spot, took him as his blood brother.

For months Hugh had been with the chief's band—living in tepees when the tribe was traveling, sleeping in snug earth-covered lodges in the winter. He'd learned Indian ways, learned how they hunted, learned how to use a bow, and had even gone on war parties with them, carrying the rifle that Chief Black Elk had given him. It was mighty like that old flintlock of his father's—same make, same true aim. He'd come to call it Old Faithful.

When Chief Black Elk had taken him along to St. Louis last winter for a big powwow with the government people, he'd left the Pawnees and joined up with Ashley and the Rocky Mountain Fur Company. That had led up to the fight with the Rees . . . and then the grizzly bear.

The vision of that fight with the great white bear brought him back to consciousness. Sweat dripped from him. He tossed, he groaned. He remembered Jim Bridger above him, fixing his bandages, feeding him soup. "'Tain't no use," he heard someone say. "He can't eat, can't talk, and seems like he's burnin' up with fever. He's gonna die."

"Not me!" Hugh told himself. "Takes more than an old she-grizzly to kill this hoss."

Then another voice—Fitz. "If those Rees had spotted us, it would've been curtains," he was saying. "We gotta get out of here pronto. No use all of us dyin'."

"But we can't just leave Hugh," Jim was saying. "Not while he's still alive."

The tangled images tumbled and tossed about in Hugh's fevered brain. He felt as though he was burning up.

"Water, Jim—give me some water," he tried to say. Only gurgling sounds came from his torn throat. Rivulets of sweat ran down his nose and dripped onto his chin. His mind went blank, and once again he was unconscious.

He heard a bird singing, far away. The notes sounded over and over, cascading into his ears. A meadowlark, his mind told him as he struggled toward consciousness. A rosy yellow light glowed on the inner surface of his closed eyelids. With an effort he opened them. Blue sky above and a pattern of chokecherry leaves. A fresh breeze ruffled the leaves. The bright sun warmed the blanket and the sandy soil on which he lay.

Where am I? Hugh asked himself. He tried to get up, but fell back with an anguished cry. Dried blood had glued his back to the blanket. The effort to rise had ripped the wounds open and started them bleeding again.

For a few moments he lay motionless, panting from the

Grizzly bear. America's most dangerous game animal, the grizzly is universally respected. "The wonderful power of life which these animals possess renders them dreadful," explorer Meriwether Lewis recorded in his journals. "We had rather encounter two indians than meet a single brown bear."

waves of pain, sweat dripping off his face and chin. Slowly the agony faded. Memories of what had happened flooded back. Waugh! That bear had really done a job on him! After that fight, everything was all jumbled in his mind.

Dimly he recalled Major Henry and Black Harris peering down at him. They were sewing up his wounds. He touched his throat, gingerly fingered the torn flesh and crude stitches. The same with his scalp and thigh. What that she-devil of a grizzly had done to his back and behind he could only imagine from the feel of the raw flesh. Ah well, the boys had done their best for him.

He remembered Fitz and young Jim looking after him—at least some of it. He reckoned he'd been out of touch and delirious a lot of the time. He recalled the fever, the torture of the poisoned raw wounds.

Groaning, he lifted a finger to his forehead. Cool. The fever had broken at last. You're a tough old hoss, Hugh, he said to himself. It'll take more than Old Ephraim to put you down.

But where are the boys? he asked himself. What he needed now was water. His lips felt dry and cracked, and his throat seemed full of cotton. His very soul cried out for water.

"Jim," he whispered, "where are you? Give Old Hugh some water now." He groaned as he looked around. No one in sight. Jim and Fitz must be off getting food. The others must have gone on to the Yellowstone. Only sensible thing to do, with the country swarming with Rees. But Jim and Fitz had stayed to look after him . . . hadn't they?

He felt a sudden quiver of uncertainty. What if they'd gone hunting and the Indians had jumped them? Poor Jim and Fitz! But suppose it had happened? What sort of fix did that leave him in? After what that bear had done to him, he sure wasn't going anywhere very quick.

Now wide awake, he cautiously raised his head and looked about. Under a cottonwood tree some twenty feet away, he saw a pile of dirt and stones beside a big hole in the ground. The boys had been digging. But why? Nothing to dig for here. Then the truth suddenly hit him. They'd been digging a grave for Old Hugh. They thought he'd be going under! But he'd fool them.

He looked down on the bloodstained blanket on which he had been lying and groped at his side to feel for his rifle. It wasn't there. He felt for his bullet pouch, his powder horn. Gone. Dagnab it—what had the boys done with them?

Just a few feet away were the remains of a small fire. Groaning, he crawled over to it and cautiously thrust his hand into the ashes. Cold. That fire had been out for at least a couple of days. There was no pot—nothing, in fact, besides himself and the blanket.

An almost unbelievable possibility dawned on him. Had his two *compañeros* deserted him, taking all his belongings with them? He shook his head in disbelief. But then the voices and memories came back . . . Fitz arguing. "C'mon, we're leavin' right now." And Jim's answer. "You ain't takin' his rifle and all his fixin's, are you?" Their voices arguing. Then silence.

Hugh thought hard. "His rifle and all his fixin's. . ." Now he was certain he had been abandoned. There was no other answer to it. He'd been left to die by those two he thought were friends. They'd lit out to save their own hides, not even leaving him his rifle or knife.

Black anger welled up in him. Well, he'd show those two. He wasn't going to die! He'd live and track down Fitz and Jim if it was the last thing he ever did. He'd get his revenge on them. Leaving him in the wilderness with nothing—two hundred miles from the nearest trading post. Bait for the wolves or the first party of Indians that stumbled on him. Oh, he'd get those two faithless skunks!

Hugh tried to crawl toward the little spring, no more than twenty feet away, but the effort and the movement opened several of his wounds again. The blood began to flow. Waves of pain swept over him and he fell back, fainting from the effort.

When he woke again, he knew the fever had come back. His face and head were hot. Groaning, he inched forward toward the spring. Each movement was agony, the raw wounds scraping against the sand and rough ground, fresh blood seeping out. Gritting his teeth, he persisted—inch by inch, foot by foot.

At last he reached the little spring and thrust his head into it. He drank greedily. "Whoa there, hoss," he muttered. "Don't take too much all at once or you'll founder."

Reluctantly he let up. A bit at a time, he thought. But those few swallows made him feel better. Advancing another few feet, he crawled right into the shallow creek and let the cool water soak through his bloody buckskins and bandages. He ducked his head, then lifted and shook it. The cold water treatment felt good. Finally he crawled onto the grassy bank and fell asleep, the warm sun beaming down on him.

5
Start of the Crawl

Dawn was just breaking when Hugh Glass wakened. He was stiff and sore, and every bone in his body ached. But the fever seemed to have gone. He touched his wounds gingerly. They weren't bleeding, he noted with relief.

He crawled back to the spring and drank deeply. Water. Every living thing needed water to live. Needed food, too, he thought. Suddenly he felt ravenous. He hadn't eaten anything at all for he didn't how many days. How long ago had those two worthless coyotes abandoned him? How long since the old she-bear had attacked him? He didn't know. All he knew was that now he was hungry.

Slowly he reached for a hanging branch of chokecherry, and his trembling fingers stripped off a handful of the berries. Thrusting them into his mouth he chewed them, spitting out the pits and swallowing the tart pulp with relish. Ah! Good. He stripped other nearby branches of berries and ate them, too. Then, exhausted, he went back to sleep.

For the next several days he lay on the bank of the spring, sleeping most of the time. When he was awake he ate chokecherries and the few wild plums within reach, then soaked his torn body in the sandy shallows. The cold water did as much good as anything, he figured, to help the healing.

One morning a crusty scab on his shoulder came off, and he noted that a tissue-thin layer of skin was beginning to grow over the wound. He felt a glow of satisfaction. An hour later, however, he felt the healing tissue on his shoulder tear. He had moved too suddenly, had stretched the tender new skin too much. As for his ripped-up back and rear, they were in worse shape. Flies kept buzzing about the gaping hole on his back, which was still open and festering. That ragged buckskin shirt of his was so torn it didn't give much protection.

He tried several times to get to his feet, but he couldn't. That gimpy leg of his had been slashed to the bone by the old she-grizzly. Maybe the leg was broken, or maybe he was just too weak to stand up.

If he could just get something more than berries to eat, he thought. Berries went through a body like a dose of salts. What he really needed was some red meat. But where to get it? He couldn't move, he had no weapons. And Fort Kiowa, the nearest place for help, was close to two hundred miles away as the crow flies. There was a chill nip in the night air now. He had lost track of the days, but it felt like September.

As he dozed by the spring that morning, he felt a slight movement along his side. A mouse? Then he felt a weight being dragged over his outstretched arm. Heavy. Rough and scaly, too.

Turning his head, he saw a big prairie rattlesnake crawling slowly over his arm. It seemed lethargic—probably because of the chilly night temperature. Hugh lay rigid, scarcely daring to breathe as the venomous reptile slithered on another few feet toward a rock outthrust. There it stretched out, soaking up heat from the surface warmed by the morning sun. About time for it to go underground for the winter, Hugh thought. But here it was, food for the taking. Meat's meat, whether it's buffalo or snake.

Extending his right arm very slowly, Hugh groped with his fingers for a rock to use as a weapon. Finally his hand closed around a fist-sized stone about the shape of an axe head. Grasping it firmly, he began to inch his way toward the snake. The big reptile lay motionless, the only sign of life being its narrow forked tongue which flicked in and out every few moments, testing the air.

Crawling to within three feet of the snake and holding his breath, Hugh raised his stone weapon. The snake did not move. Down came his arm as the stone smashed into the head of the rattlesnake. The thick yellow-and-tan body thrashed and coiled as Hugh struck it repeatedly until he was certain that the snake was dead.

Exhausted by his effort, Hugh lay back for a few minutes until he felt able to continue. Then, using the edge of the stone, he sawed at the snake's neck until he finally cut off its head. It was slow going; he needed a better knife.

Looking around, he spotted a small flat stone near the spring. Crawling over, he picked it up and examined it. It had a sharp cutting edge. The next best thing to a steel knife, he told himself. Using the primitive tool, Hugh hacked at the underbelly of the snake, starting where he had cut off the head. The splotched yellow scales were wide and surprisingly tough, but they yielded to the stone's cutting edge. Hugh peeled off the scaly skin, exposing the snake's white flesh.

Ah, if he just had a little fire to grill that rattlesnake meat, he thought, it'd be better. But he had no flint or steel to start a fire. Tearing off a small piece of snake meat, he chewed and finally swallowed the stringy flesh.

He grimaced as he swallowed it. It would taste better if it was roasted, but raw rattlesnake was better than nothing. He ate more of the pale white flesh, then sank back, exhausted. In a few minutes he was asleep.

When he woke up—how many hours later he didn't know—he felt better. Waugh! That snake meat had done something for him. Better than eating berries. He crawled over to the spring for a drink, then forced down another meal of raw reptilian flesh. After soaking his wounds in the cold water, he crawled up onto the sun-warmed bank and slept once again.

For the next five days Hugh Glass remained by the spring, alternately sleeping, eating rattler meat and berries, soaking his wounds in the cold water, and drying off in the warm midday sunshine. Gradually he gained strength. He saw that scabs had formed over many of his open wounds. But his body was still stiff and sore, and it seemed as if every joint ached.

In the early nineteenth century, wolves ranged throughout the West. Following the buffalo, they preyed on calves and on infirm or aged specimens.

One morning he was wakened by a pressure on the blanket which covered him. Something was tugging at it, trying to pull it off him. Struggling out of sleep, he opened his eyes and looked directly into the face of a wolf. The pale eyes glowed as they gazed at him from less than two feet away. The beast's furry muzzle and cheeks were straw-colored, the pointed ears and lips rimmed with black.

Hugh rolled away, and the wolf vanished in an instant. Raising himself on one arm, he saw the big wild dog some distance away, loping toward a spot on the prairie where three other wolves waited.

"Time to get goin', old hoss," Hugh muttered to himself. "Walk or not, ye gotta get outta here—else the wolves or the Rees'll get ye." Groaning, he pulled himself over to where the dismembered rattlesnake lay. He could barely stand the smell of it anymore, but it had kept him alive so far. He swallowed some of the rancid flesh for breakfast, washing it down with water, and finished his meal with a few chokecherries. Then he slept.

By the time he wakened, the sun was sinking toward the western horizon. The day had been warm, but as evening approached, the air had a chill nip to it. There'd be frost most any day. Time to head for help, Hugh told himself. He needed to get a rifle and other fixin's so he could start tracking down those two varmints who had deserted him. Every time he thought of Fitz and Jim he could feel the anger welling up in him, bitter as gall. Taking Old Faithful and all his gear and leaving him to die! Any man who was a man wouldn't do that to a dog. Ah, he'd make them pay, he would, once he got out of this fix. He had to get out of here, had to get some help.

But where to go? None of the possibilities looked very good. He sure as shooting couldn't make it to Henry's post on the Yellowstone—too far north, and he didn't know that country. And if he tried heading back along the Grand River to the Big Muddy, he'd like as not run into a war party of Arikaras. Not that the country would be safe in any direction, for only God knew where the Indians had scattered to.

His best bet, he decided, was to head southeast for Fort Kiowa, even if it was nearly two hundred miles away. Could he make it? He didn't know, but he'd sure try.

The way to do it, Hugh thought, was to strike straight

out for the fort, traveling at night and keeping close to cover and to the little gullies and creeks where he could find water and a few trees—cottonwoods or willows—to hide out in and sleep under during the day.

He immediately began to make himself ready for the long trip as best he could. Tearing off some strips of his blanket, he bound them to his knees and elbows with some of the leather fringes from his buckskin shirt. He stuffed the remaining morsels of rattlesnake flesh inside his shirt. Finally, he rolled up his tattered and bloody blanket and fastened it across his shoulders.

Where the blanket had lain, he found a prize—his little bag of possibles. Those miserable coyotes had overlooked that when they left. Nothing much of value, he thought—his old pipe, a bit of tobacco, a few bright beads from his Pawnee days. Then he gasped with delight as he emptied the bag. There was a flint and steel! He'd forgotten about them. Fixin's for a fire. And better yet, the old razor that had been his father's. Now he'd be able not only to make fire but to skin any varmint he might be lucky enough to catch, and to cut it up for meat, too.

The sun was just setting as Hugh Glass started off, crawling painfully away from the spring and up onto the bare prairie. He headed for a gully he could see a half mile or more to the southeast. It was overgrown with scrub.

Hugh felt every rock as he pulled himself over the ground, felt the prickly grass brush against his torn face and neck. A warm dampness spread across his leg. Some of the scabs had scraped off, he reckoned, and the wounds were open again. He'd bled so much recently that he thought more than once he couldn't have much blood left in him. Still, it kept coming out.

He groaned a bit, then crawled on, foot by foot, yard by yard. He winced as one groping hand came down on the spines of a prickly pear cactus. Better that, though, than on another rattler. Soon, however, it would be too cold for critters like them to be about.

After what seemed like many hours, the moon was high overhead and Hugh was exhausted. He looked back. Hadn't moved more than a quarter mile. The stars were bright in the sky and the moon cast a silvery sheen over the grassland. Behind him, he heard coyotes yapping; then, in the distance, the mournful chorus of a pack of wolves on the hunt. He gazed ahead at the scrubby coulee that was his goal. It seemed as far away as when he'd first started out.

Hours later, he still had a piece to go before he'd be at that scrub-covered draw. He was about done in, he admitted to himself. Couldn't go much farther tonight. By now the moon had set and he was surrounded by the cold predawn darkness. He crawled doggedly on. A thin streak of light rimmed the eastern horizon. Soon it would be daylight. He would still be out in the open, where any Rees might find him. Gritting his teeth, he kept going.

Dawn was just breaking when Hugh finally made it to the shelter of the coulee. Crawling through the border of scrub willows, he slid down the steep sandy bank to the place where a tiny rivulet of water flowed between the eroded sides. After drinking his fill, he ate a few morsels of the stringy rattlesnake meat and grimaced. It was turning bad.

Completely exhausted, he crept into a sheltered hiding place under the low-spreading willows, wrapped himself in the tattered remnants of his blanket, and slept.

6

Wolves and Buffalo

Hugh Glass was awakened by a buzzing sound—at first faint, then louder and louder. He felt a tickling in his right ear as a mosquito landed on it. Hugh grunted irritably as it took off, circling his nose and then landing on his torn scalp. He brushed it away.

Every muscle in his body ached. That crawl last night had almost done him in. A half mile! Only 199½ to go! He groaned. Would he ever make it?

Whoa, old hoss, he cautioned himself. Quit thinking like that. You'll make it. You've got to make it so you can get back at those thieving skunks that robbed you and left you to die. Suddenly Hugh felt the bitter anger welling up within him once again, like a smoldering volcano ready to erupt. He pounded the ground with his fist in sheer frustration, then gazed skyward. "God be my witness," he cried out. "I swear I'll track down them varmints and make 'em pay fer their sins. Revenge is mine! An eye fer an eye . . . a tooth fer a tooth . . ."

Exhausted, he sank back, trembling, his heart thumping, hot hammers pounding inside his head. Gradually the trembling stopped, and his heart slowed back to normal. Ah, he thought, no good to get worked up like that . . . it feels mighty queersome. Better I save my strength for what lies ahead.

He peered out of his little brush-covered hiding place by the stream. It was still daylight, but the sun was low. Far off he heard the familiar sound of wolves howling. After a kill of buffalo or deer, likely. Ah-h-h, what he wouldn't do to get some meat!

As he sat up, he heard a snort behind him. Turning, he glimpsed a big whitetail buck as it leaped across the stream and took off. He'd startled it. If only I had a rifle, he thought.

Another mosquito hummed about his head. Then a big grasshopper landed with clicking wings just two feet from his side. Cupping his hand, Hugh made a quick sweep and captured it. Pulling of its head, wings, and hind legs, he quickly put the rest of the grasshopper into his mouth and crunched down. Better than nothing, he told himself. As a matter of fact, it wasn't bad. It tasted rather like chestnuts. He realized how hungry he was.

He took out the remains of the rattlesnake and tried a

bit of it. He grimaced, then spit it out and threw the rest away. Too far gone, even for someone as hungry as he was. He picked a few chokecherries and ate them, together with a couple of wild turnips that he dug up with a sharp rock. Not very satisfactory, but something, at least. Time to get going again.

That night Hugh crawled nearly two miles. Not far. He was able to do more than that in half an hour when he was healthy, but it was better than the night before. He followed the creek bed most of the way, with big Thunder Butte, far to the southeast, beckoning him on. When he finally passed it, he'd be close to the Moreau River. The creek he was following would probably lead him right to it.

Night after night, day after day, he crawled southward. Soon he was doing much of his traveling during daylight hours. Riskier, perhaps, but he always kept close to the shelter of the trees and bushes along the streambed, and searched for food along the way.

Sometimes he advanced as much as four or five miles in twenty-four hours, sometimes only half that much. Most of his wounds—even that torn throat of his—were mending, with layers of new skin closing over them, except for the one on his back where the grizzly had raked the flesh right down to the bone. He couldn't reach that spot with his fingers, but he was sure that it was still raw and open. Flies were constantly buzzing around it.

He still couldn't do much more than crawl along on his hands and knees, mostly because of that game leg. Had that old grizzly cracked or broken the bones? They seemed to fit together all right, but he couldn't put any weight on

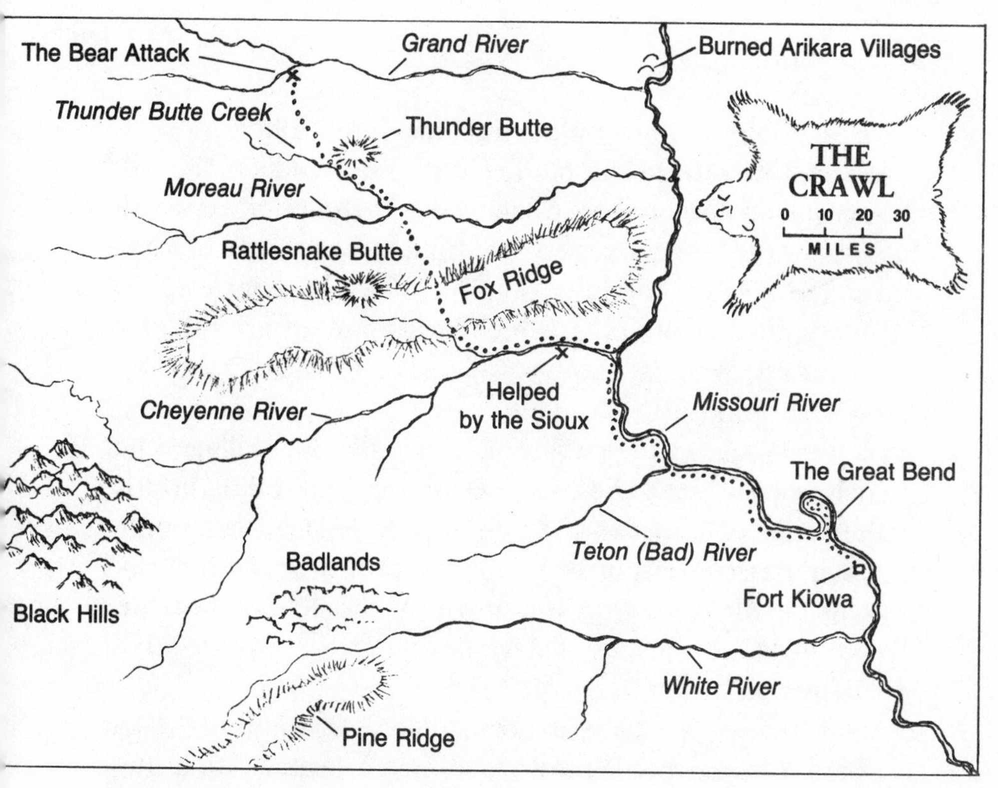

Map showing the route of the crawl.

the leg. Just trying to stand up was too much of an effort. Even if he had a crutch he couldn't have done it. Too weak. What he needed was some real food—buffalo or venison—real red meat. A meal like that would go far to make up for all the blood he'd lost.

After a week of crawling, Hugh lost track of the passage of time. Day succeeded day, always the same test of pain, endurance, hunger—especially hunger. Water, although sometimes only a pool of stagnant water in the almost dry streambed, was no problem. Food was. But he survived. The time he'd spent as the adopted brother of a Pawnee chief was paying off. Because of that, he knew which plants had edible roots or bulbs, he knew how to find food, no matter how bare the land. He dug up wild onion, wild turnip, and other roots to gnaw on. He found the few wild plums and late chokecherries still left. Every time he came across a rotten log he tore into it like a bear, in search of fat, white beetle grubs, which he swallowed greedily. But he really wanted red meat. Even a mouse would taste mighty good.

One day he came upon a prairie dog village that stretched as far as he could see on the high rolling prairie. He saw a number of the plump little rodents rising up at their burrow entrances to look about, their short black-tipped tails jerking up and down. At the sight of him, they shrilled loud whistles of alarm, then darted down into their burrows.

A small owl stood in front of one of the burrows. It blinked as he crawled toward it, then retreated into its nest hole. Burrowing owls often shared prairie dog homes, as Hugh knew. He'd seen them in many dog towns.

A few minutes later a sleek weasel-like animal darted past Hugh and disappeared down a prairie dog hole. Moments later it reappeared, carrying a plump young prairie dog in its mouth. The victim was still alive, Hugh observed, and was making faint squeaking noises as the big weasel disappeared into the prairie grass.

"Now what in tarnation would that critter be?" Hugh asked himself. "Big as a mink, but honey-colored, and with black feet and a black mask across its eyes. Whatever it be, I wish I could be as quick as it is. Then I'd catch m'self a prairie dog fer my supper."

Hugh spent the better part of the afternoon trying. Fashioning a lasso of buckskin from the fringes of his tattered hunting shirt, he encircled a hole with the noose and lay back, waiting patiently. When a little rodent finally popped out of the burrow, however, he jerked his lasso too late. The dog yipped with alarm as it whisked off, free as a bird. Hugh tried again and again, but with no better luck.

Weary and disgusted, he finally gave up. Crawling back to the creek, he sucked the good out of a few wild plums that he found and then began to search for roots or other vegetable matter. Turning over a flat rock in the shallow water, he spied two crayfish, each about three inches long. With a quick thrust of his hand, he scooped up both of them.

He grunted with satisfaction as he pulled the outer shells off the pink flesh and took his first bite. A mouthful of crayfish was a welcome change.

The next day he uncovered another source of nourishment—a cache of ground beans and other seeds that a busy field mouse had put in its underground storage chamber. These, together with a few wild peas and rose hips, were his main meal of the day. They sustained life, he told himself, but, as always, meat was what he craved.

It must be mid-September by now, Hugh figured. Perhaps later. Soon there would be frosty nights, and who knew what else. Winter was on the way, and he hadn't covered a quarter of the distance to Fort Kiowa. What he needed was real food—and good legs to walk on. He was doing five or six miles a day, he judged, but that wasn't enough.

One day he came upon the remains of a buffalo, evidently killed by wolves. They'd eaten most of the carcass, and vultures and coyotes had finished off the rest. Not long ago, judging by the remnants of putrid flesh still clinging to some of the bones. In spite of the smell, Hugh seized a rock and cracked some of the largest bones. Inside, he found some marrow. Scraping it out with a sharp stick, he mixed it with berries and mashed it into a sort of pemmican, which he quickly gobbled down.

The next day he reached the Moreau River, the one into which Thunder Butte Creek emptied. The Moreau was only about fifty feet wide at this spot, and the water was low. There had been little rain this summer and fall. Lucky in some ways, unlucky in others.

Crawling into the sluggish stream at a sandy ford, Hugh started toward the other side. In midstream, the water depth went to three or four feet. He had to swim. Striking out weakly, he found to his amazement that he could. When he reached the far bank, he crawled ashore and lay back, panting and exhausted.

No strength in him! He was weak—too weak. He gazed angrily at his scarred legs. Useless things! Meat was what he needed—red meat.

From time to time during his long crawl, he had spotted bands of buffalo in the distance or pronghorns bounding over a rise. And he'd surprised a deer or two coming to drink from the creek. But there was no way he could get any of them—not without his rifle.

He watched a pair of pintail ducks swimming downriver. A couple of brown cranes stalked through the shallows, searching for fish. Ah-h-h-h, if only he could get one of those birds. He watched longingly as they disappeared around a bend. Now, if it were springtime, he could find some nests and eggs. Sighing, he moved over to the bushes and gathered some chokecherries. Poor fare, but even berries and wild plums were almost gone. Too late in the season.

Nigh onto October, Hugh reflected. Must be three weeks or more since he'd started the crawl, and in all that time he'd advanced maybe fifty or sixty miles. Still a long way to go!

He slept that night close to the banks of the Moreau. The next morning, he woke to the sound of snarls, then a loud bawling sound, almost like a scream. It was a cry of panic and despair. Crawling to the edge of the coulee, he peered out onto the prairie. There, not two hundred yards away, was a pack of six wolves, circling around a wounded buffalo calf. They had caught this one away from its band and were aiming to finish it off.

First one wolf and then another dashed in, nipping and snapping in turn at the defenseless calf. The leader, a big wolf and lighter in color than the others, leaped for a throat hold. The calf bleated a strangled cry as it fell. In an instant the other wolves were on it, too. After a few moments the calf was dead.

The big wild dogs tore into the belly of their quarry and began to eat, snarling at one another over the division of the spoils. Hugh watched, his mouth dry, as the wolves gorged on the steaming flesh. He had to have some of that meat for himself, he thought, but the wolves might have their own ideas about that. If he was up and healthy, he'd soon make them skeedaddle. But now he was as weak as a pup, unable even to stand up. Better wait a bit, he reckoned, until the whole pack has a good feed.

Unaware of the man watching them, the wolves tore at the calf's carcass and ate until their bellies bulged. Finally they showed signs of slowing down. Easier to scare off now, Hugh thought. He shuffled forward on his hands and knees, yelling at the top of his lungs. He was surprised to hear his own voice once again. Picking up a rock, he threw it at the wolves.

Startled, the big wild dogs stopped eating and stared at Hugh, their pale eyes glowing, as he advanced slowly toward them. As he came ever closer, they snarled and bared their fangs. Making a supreme effort, Hugh stood up on his good leg for a moment. Reluctantly, the wolves backed away. They had fed well, and they hesitated to attack a man—especially a standing man. It might have been different, Hugh thought, as he slowly sank back to his crawling position. He was surprised that he'd been able to stand up, even for that brief time. As he approached the kill, the coyotes and vultures that had already gathered to await their turn at the carcass also retreated.

The wolves had eaten a large portion of the buffalo calf, but there was still plenty left. Trembling as he sank down, Hugh tore off some of the ragged edges of red meat in the underparts and stuffed them into his mouth. He chewed the still warm flesh and swallowed it. He could almost feel the blood from the red meat coursing through his veins. He gulped down more raw meat until his immediate hunger was satisfied. Finally he lay back with a great sigh of satisfaction. He felt stronger already. Now he'd cook some of the meat and eat like a human being.

Getting out his razor, he cut off as much of the remaining meat as he could carry and crawled back to the river with it. There, he gathered together a pile of dried grass and twigs of dead sagebrush. He would risk a little fire, risk the danger of any Indians nearby. Using his flint and razor, he finally got a tiny flame going and quickly fed it with larger sticks. Cutting the meat into thin slices, he propped them over the fire. Soon a delicious aroma filled the air.

He ate until he could eat no more. Finished at last, he crawled back to the carcass. After chasing the wolves away a second time, he again cut off as much meat as he could carry with him back to the river. That night he slept better than he had for many days and woke up feeling healthier than he had at any time since the bear had attacked him. Aye, he was going to make it!

7

Helped by the Sioux

Hugh stayed near the buffalo carcass for four days, eating his fill of meat, gaining strength with every mouthful. Much of the remaining flesh he cut into thin strips which he hung up to cure in the sun. When he judged the sun-dried flesh was ready, he pounded it into powder with a rock hammer, then mixed it with a few late chokecherries to make some pemmican.

In spite of all he could do to guard the carcass, the wolves visited it by night. Within a couple of days there was little left of it except bones. Hugh and the wolves left these for the coyotes and vultures that were ever watching and waiting. Crows and magpies cleaned up the last scraps.

It must be October by now, Hugh figured. October, the moon of falling leaves. The cottonwoods bordering the stream were yellow against the bright blue of the fall sky. Every time there was a breeze their leaves swirled down in a golden shower. One morning he heard honking overhead and looked up to see a flock of geese flying in a long, wavering V-formation. They were heading south.

That night there was a frosty nip to the night air, and Hugh shivered under his tattered blanket. Time for him to be heading on south, too, he reflected—south to the Cheyenne River. Then on to the Missouri and Fort Kiowa. But before he started, he'd make himself a crutch. It'd be some use to him, now that he knew he could stand. He'd surprised himself when he found he could do it, even though just for a moment, when he drove the wolves away from the carcass of the buffalo calf. Since he'd stood up once, he could do it again—and with a crutch he might be able to stay up and hobble along.

The next morning he crawled over to a nearby cottonwood tree that had been laid open and killed by lightning. After carefully checking the possibilities, he finally selected a stout limb with a right-angled crook where it joined a larger limb. Working slowly and carefully, he cut the limb off with his razor. After smoothing the end with the crook in it, he lay on his back and tucked that end under his arm. Measuring by eye, he noted where the other end met his foot. He then cut the crutch to length.

Hugh looked at the crude finished product with a feeling of satisfaction. Maybe—just maybe—he could walk a bit with its help.

Cautiously shifting to a sitting position, he grasped the trunk of a young aspen with his left hand and tried to stand on his good left leg. At last he was in an upright position for the first time since he had stood for that brief moment against the wolves. Tucking his handmade crutch under his right arm, he gingerly tried putting a little weight on the lame right leg. He winced at the stab of sharp pain. Not yet. Not yet. But perhaps he could navigate without putting any weight on that leg. He tried. One step, then two. He found that he could limp slowly ahead. At least it was better than crawling.

With his crutch he would be able to go eight or ten miles a day, he figured. He'd lost track of days, but he had been crawling, he thought, for close to three weeks before he came upon the buffalo calf. And before that—how long had he been lying where Fitz and Jim had left him for dead? Anger burned within him at the thought. He'd make it to Fort Kiowa yet. He'd get himself outfitted and go after those two. All he had to do was to keep from starving—and he'd do that. He'd made out so far!

Before he started off with his new crutch, however, he had one or two other things to do. Stripping off his tattered, blood-encrusted clothes, he scrubbed them with wet sand at the edge of the creek, then rinsed and laid them out to dry in the afternoon sun. Next, he crawled into the stream and washed himself all over as best he could. New pink skin, he noted, was now growing over most of his wounds—except for that open wound on his back that he couldn't reach. From the feel of it—and the smell—it was still open and infected. He rubbed his back on the sandy bottom of the river, trying to clean out the wound, but the sudden, searing pain made him feel faint. Ah-h-h-h, enough of that! He'd get it attended to once he got to Fort Kiowa.

Crawling out on the bank, he lay down and let his bare body soak in the rays of the sun, now directly overhead. When his tattered clothes were dry, he put them back on. For the first time since the bear attack, he felt almost human once again. Time to be on his way.

It was late afternoon by now, and the October air was noticeably cooler. Hugh ate the last of the fresh buffalo meat and tucked the cakes of pemmican into a pocket of the shirt. Putting his handmade crutch under his right arm, he started off, taking care to put as little weight as possible on the wounded leg.

After sunset, a full moon lighted the way as he left the river and headed southeast toward the gentle rising hills that made up Fox Ridge. He would have to cross those hills before he could make his way down into the valley of the Cheyenne River—some forty miles away, he guessed.

Ahead of him to the west was Rattlesnake Butte. When he passed it, he would be over Fox Ridge and halfway to the Cheyenne. Then he'd hit a creek that ran right into her, he told himself. Every step was bringing him farther into the country of the Sioux, and that was good. The Dakotas, as they called themselves, were generally friendly to mountain men and other whites, and had helped in the campaign against the Rees.

By dawn Hugh figured he had done a good eight miles. He holed up for the day in a small, almost dry ravine rimmed with low willows. Just a trickle of water came down from the higher land ahead, but it was enough. He drank and then ate a few mouthfuls of his meat-berry mixture. Then he slept.

It took three days for him to reach and cross over the

highlands of Fox Ridge. From that point on, it was easier going as he started down, following a tiny brook that meandered southward through the flat prairie. Far in the distance he could see the trees that signaled the valley of the Cheyenne River. By now, Rattlesnake Butte was far behind him, on the western horizon. The next day he reached the Cheyenne itself. The river was low, its waters sluggish and clear.

He had been lucky so far, he reflected. All this way, and no murdering Rees. Now he was in Sioux country, and if he ran into any Indians they'd probably be friendly.

He spotted several catfish in the shallows of the river and with a sharpened stick managed to spear two of them. That night he dined on broiled fish, with wild onions for greens, all washed down with clear river water.

Since he was in wooded land beside the river, he decided to travel most of the time by day as he headed eastward to where the Cheyenne flowed into the Missouri. After two days, he figured he wasn't more than another day's journey from the Big Muddy. He was getting close to his goal—close to the time when he could go after Jim Bridger and that other worthless character, John Fitzgerald.

As he rounded a bend in the river that afternoon, he heard a horse nickering ahead of him. As fast as he could, he hobbled toward a thicket of underbrush to hide. But he was too late. A half dozen mounted Indians cantered into view, several of them leading pack horses loaded down with bulging baskets and rawhide bags. They were Sioux, Hugh noted immediately, not Rees, as he had feared at first.

At the sight of him the horsemen reined abruptly, and

two of them covered him with their rifles. He quickly extended his hand in a sign of peace, then spread both his arms, palms up, to show that he had no weapons. He had learned a few words of the Sioux language when the Indians and the mountain men had marched together against the Rees. Before he could say anything, however, the Sioux leader spoke to him in halting English. Who was he? What was his business?

Using a combination of words and sign language, Hugh explained what had happened during the past few weeks. No sense in saying he'd been deserted and left for dead, he decided. That was private business between him and his two *compañeros*. Instead, he related how he had become separated from Major Henry's party after the Arikara campaign. Then the desperate fight with the grizzly and how he had lain like dead for days until he had gathered enough strength to begin his crawl. Now he was headed for Fort Kiowa.

The Indians gathered around him, and Hugh heard their sharp intakes of breath as they examined the many marks of his fight with the grizzly. Taking off his shirt, he showed them the festering wound on his back.

"The great white bear is a mighty fighter," observed the Sioux leader as he took in the extent of Hugh's injuries, "but any man who kills a white bear is a greater fighter. Badger and his warriors salute you, a killer of bears."

To the Sioux, the grizzly bear was an almost sacred animal that they feared and venerated. Any man who killed one in hand-to-hand combat was a mighty warrior.

Badger then told Hugh how he and the warriors of his village had fought in the campaign against the Arikaras, too. Now they were on their way home from the site of the burned Ree villages, where they had gone to harvest corn and squash from the deserted fields. He waved at the pack horses, loaded with produce. They were on their way back to their own village. It was just a few miles away, he said. They would take Hugh with them and see to it that he got down to Fort Kiowa safely.

Two of the warriors unloaded a pack horse and distributed its burden among the other horses. Then they helped Hugh onto its back. He winced with pain as he sat astride the Indian pony. The bite the bear had taken out of his behind was still mighty tender, and this critter he was on must have a ridged backbone.

The party set out at once. His mount's movement over the rough ground made Hugh groan at times, but he clung to the rawhide reins and tried to think of brighter days ahead.

It was late afternoon when they came in sight of the Sioux village—a cluster of twenty or more hide tepees in a small clearing near the river. As the party rode into the village they were greeted by a chorus of barking dogs—yelping first in excitement and then in welcome. Black-eyed children peeked out at Hugh from behind the hide-covered dwellings, and the women looked up from their work, their faces showing pleasure at the return of their men. The full loads on the pack horses told them that a good harvest of Arikara corn, squash, and pumpkins had been gathered, too.

Reining up in front of his tepee, Badger directed his men to distribute the produce to everyone in the village. Helping Hugh to dismount, he beckoned him into his lodge.

Sioux village, after a painting by Karl Bodmer. Note the funeral scaffold of a chief. Rather than bury their dead, the Sioux and other Plains Indians lashed the remains on elevated scaffolds or in trees. When only bones were left, they were placed in rock crevices.

"First we eat," he announced, motioning to Hugh to sit down beside him on a buffalo robe. "Then my wives will take care of your back."

Hugh nodded. It would be good to get that pesky back looked at. He glanced at Badger's two women, who were cutting up some fresh venison and adding it to a large pot that was simmering over a small fire in the center of the lodge. One was slim and comely, he noted, while the other was quite a bit older, and thick about the middle. Both of the women cast shy sideways glances at their visitor as they added wild onions, squash, and corn to the pot. A delicious aroma soon began to fill the tepee. In the dim recesses of the lodge opposite him, Hugh could see an old woman, white-haired, wrinkled, and toothless. Hunched

Portrait of an Oglala Sioux chief, Matau-Tathonca (Bull Bear), as painted by Alfred Jacob Miller.

in an ancient robe, she stared impassively at him, silent and motionless. The mother of one of Badger's wives, Hugh reckoned. Beside her were three small children—a boy and two girls—who were watching, round-eyed.

After a few moments, three Sioux warriors came into

the lodge. After offering their greetings, they sat down, cross-legged, around the fire. Badger then filled a long ceremonial pipe with tobacco and lighted it. Waving it in turn to the sky, the earth, and the four great directions, he took a long draw on it, exhaled the thin blue smoke, and then passed it on to Hugh. The mountain man drew on the pipe in turn, and passed it on to the man next to him. By the time it had made the rounds of all of them, the meal was ready.

Dipping buffalo horn ladles into the common pot, the Sioux warriors scooped out pieces of meat and vegetables that they heaped into wooden bowls. Immediately they began to shovel the food into their mouths with their fingers, accompanying every dripping mouthful with approving smacks of their lips and enthusiastic licks of their fingers.

Hugh, in his turn, dipped his ladle into the pot and filled it with broth, thick with firm pieces of venison and chunks of squash. Never, he thought, had food tasted so good. He ate until he felt he could eat no more. Finished, he sighed with satisfaction and gave a loud belch of appreciation. Badger's women tittered, and even Badger and the other warriors smiled.

After the visitors had left, Badger indicated to Hugh that he should strip down so that his wives could wash his clothes and mend those that warranted it. They would treat his back wound as well.

When Hugh took off his buckskin shirt, the two women gasped as they examined the open wound on his back. "It full of worms," Badger explained to Hugh. But it was a good thing, he added, for the fly maggots had fed on the wound and cleaned out most of the rotten flesh. His women would take care of the rest.

Hugh lay stomach down on the buffalo robe while Badger's two wives cleaned out the wound. He winced at their touch, gentle as it was. Soon they had prepared a mixture of herbs over the fire—he couldn't tell what went into the medicine. When it was ready, they poured the hot liquid over the raw flesh. It burned like fire, making Hugh grunt. But the more it hurts, the better the medicine, he told himself. Satisfied, the women put a soothing oily salve over the wound, then bandaged it with strips of soft, tanned antelope skin. Badger grunted his approval.

"You sleep now," he told Hugh. "Tomorrow you eat and sleep some more and my women fix your back again. Make you new moccasins and shirt, too. When sun comes again, I take you to Fort Kiowa."

Hugh nodded, sighing with contentment. He'd almost forgotten how it felt to have a full belly of good cooked food and a soft robe to sleep on. He closed his eyes and in a moment was asleep.

8

Fort Kiowa at Last

After two days of eating his fill of the hearty meals provided by Badger's wives, after two days of having his back wound cleaned and treated, Hugh felt like a new man. All of his wounds were fast healing now, even that torn throat. His voice was coming back, too. It sounded different than it had before the bear fight, he admitted to himself—deeper, rather like the croak of a big bullfrog—but at least he could talk again.

Hugh felt good about his gimpy leg, too. He still needed his crutch, but for the first time he could put a little weight on that leg when he stood up. Maybe it wasn't broken after all; maybe all he'd needed was to start getting his strength back.

He would carry plenty of scars on his scalp, face, and legs for the rest of his life, but what matter. They were honorable scars, and he'd never won any prizes for his looks, anyway. Hugh grinned at the thought. He looked better, at least, than when he'd started this crawl.

He inspected the new doeskin britches and the fringed hunting shirt that Badger's wives had made for him. He wiggled his toes in the new moccasins they had given him as well. Ah, they felt good! Now he was ready to head on to Fort Kiowa.

Badger and several of his friends would be going downriver the next day to visit relatives at the Sioux settlement near the fort. They planned to take along some of the Arikara produce as gifts, as well as several bundles of skins that they would turn in for trade goods.

At sunup the next morning, Hugh settled himself in the middle of a big pirogue—a dugout canoe made from the trunk of an old cottonwood tree. Two young men with paddles got in behind him and two others in front. Nearby was a second pirogue, also with a crew of four. Both canoes were loaded with produce and bundles of furs. Hugh settled back with a contented sigh as they shoved out into the current and headed downriver.

On either side of him, the waters of the Missouri flowed silent and placid, for the river was low, the current slack. Mighty different from the boiling high waters of the spring flood season, Hugh reflected. Entirely at ease, he leaned back on a buffalo robe and watched the changing scene.

The sandy banks of the river were lined with white driftwood, with here and there a high bluff blocking off the view of the prairies beyond. In many areas the shores were bordered by thick stands of cottonwoods and willows. Most of the leaves had already fallen, but a few trees still flamed with bright yellow foliage. Tangles of wild grapevines covered many of them, making a jungle of the riverbank. Other areas were almost treeless, showing only sagebrush and prairie grasses.

They passed deer drinking in the shallows several times, and once Hugh glimpsed a band of antelope that stared at them curiously from a high bluff. When they stopped to camp that first evening, Badger and one of the others set out to hunt meat for the evening meal. Soon they returned with a young whitetail doe that Badger had shot.

That night, warm and relaxed under a blanket and buffalo robe, Hugh looked up at the stars and grunted with satisfaction. Thanks to Badger and his friends, he would be in Fort Kiowa in a couple of days—far ahead of what he had hoped. Once there, he'd get outfitted again, ready to head upriver to Henry's post on the Yellowstone. There, he would get his vengeance on those two cowards who had deserted him. A life for a life, he thought grimly. They'd left him to die. Well, he would see that they paid for their treachery. With that thought he fell asleep.

On down the wide Missouri they traveled the next day—past Cedar Island, past the mouth of the Teton or Bad River, on past great groves of giant cottonwood trees and rolling grasslands that stretched westward to the horizon, brown and golden. Several times that day they encountered other Sioux Indians in canoes. This was the heartland of the Dakota nation—the center of Sioux territory.

Typical of early western forts, with stout cottonwood palisades and two diagonally positioned blockhouses, this is Fort Laramie as seen by artist Alfred Jacob Miller in 1837. Built at the confluence of the North Platte and Laramie rivers, this post of the American Fur Company was a welcome sight for settlers traveling west on the Oregon Trail.

It was nearly noon of the second day when they came to the great bend of the Missouri, where the river curved northwest, then southeast in a great loop some thirty miles long. As it continued southward, the river passed the neck of the loop, which a man could walk across in an hour's time or less. Fort Kiowa was only a few miles away.

It was late afternoon when the pirogue rounded a bend in the river and Hugh spotted the familiar sight of the French Fur Company's post, a half mile ahead on a rise on the west bank. A stout stockade some twenty feet high, built of upright cottonwood logs, enclosed Fort Kiowa. Each of the four sides of these outer walls was about one hundred forty feet long. The only entrance was the big gate facing the river, where a sentinel always stood guard against any possible danger. Even though the fort was located in the Sioux heartland and the Dakotas were friendly, fur traders had to be on constant guard against attack from other tribes—Arikaras, Pawnees, or any number of others.

The fort had a rifle walk, fifteen feet high on the inner side of the stockade, which was usually manned by several riflemen. A big blockhouse rose at the southeast corner of the fort, facing the river. On the northwest corner there was a rifle tower that looked out over the western prairie. From these, the men inside Fort Kiowa could command a field of fire in all directions in case of attack.

The Sioux paddlers steered the two canoes over to the sandy beach beside the loading dock and dragged them up on the bank. A short distance upstream was a cluster of tepees where the Dakotas who chose to stay close to the fort lived. Badger and the others were soon unloading the pirogues, getting ready to visit their relatives.

After taking a warm departure of Badger and the other Sioux, Hugh limped over to the main gate of the fort, leaning heavily on his crutch. The Stars and Stripes waved from a high pole inside. As he approached the gate, the sentinel on guard squinted down at him.

"What's yer business, podner?" he demanded.

Hugh looked up at him. The sentinel was old Tom Flynn, with whom he'd tipped many a cup on his previous visit to the fort last spring, on the way upriver. Tom had been one of the earliest trappers on the Yellowstone, a dozen or more years ago. Now the aches and pains of age had tied him to life at the trading post. His eyes were dim, his step halting. But maybe it's me that's changed, Hugh thought.

"Don't ye know me, old hoss?" he demanded of Tom. "It's me—Hugh Glass."

The grizzled sentinel squinted down at him. "Hugh? Hugh—what in tarnation! Why, I'd niver've recognized ye. What ye doin' here, Hugh? Last I knowed—after the Ree campaign—ye was headin' fer the Yellowstone with Major Henry and his men."

"Aye, *compañero,* I was headin' fer the Yellowstone," Hugh agreed. "But I met up with a grizzly b'ar along the way, and it changed my plans a bit. So here I am back at Kiowa. Now let me in, like a good old hoss. I got some business with Young Cayewa."

Old Tom disappeared from the parapet, and a moment later the wide double gate swung open. Hobbling inside, Hugh gazed at the familiar surroundings of this principal trading post of the French Fur Company. Built the year before, it was the only trading post this far up on the Missouri until one got to the Mandan villages several hundred miles farther north, where the Columbia Fur Company had a much smaller post.

The proprietor and head man at Fort Kiowa, the bourgeois, was Joseph Brazeau, known far and wide as "Young Cayewa." He'd come into the business naturally, for his uncle—Joseph Brazeau, or "Old Cayewa"—had organized the French Fur Company and cornered most of the trade with the Sioux years before. Now Young Cayewa had built this post—and a fine one it was.

The house of the bourgeois was a stout two-storied log structure, complete with a stone chimney, directly across the parade ground from the main gate. Beside it was his clerk's quarters, and next to that a large storehouse where

This painting by Alfred Jacob Miller shows the interior of Fort Laramie as viewed from the big entrance gate looking west.

trade goods, food, and furs were stored. Along the north-facing stockade was a row of log cabins that served as quarters for the trappers, boatmen, and other employees of the company. On the opposite or southern palisade were a blacksmith shop and stables for the horses.

As he limped across the hard-packed parade ground, Hugh greeted several trappers he had met on previous visits. Then he headed toward the clerk's quarters. General Ashley had left a great store of materials here when he'd come down to the fort after the Arikara campaign. Hugh intended to outfit himself and get everything he needed from that store. After all, he was still under contract to

Ashley and the Rocky Mountain Fur Company, so he was entitled to it. He needed a whole new set of supplies before he headed on for the Yellowstone and that reckoning with Bridger and Fitz.

Before he even reached the clerk's office, he saw Young Cayewa, the bourgeois, as he was leaving his quarters. Brazeau stopped as he saw Hugh limping toward him.

"He don't know me either," Hugh told himself. Then he saw the bourgeois's eyes widen in sudden recognition.

"Glass—Hugh Glass?" he exclaimed. "What brings you here? I thought you'd gone to the Yellowstone with Henry." Coming closer, he noticed the vivid scars on Hugh's face and throat.

"*Mon Dieu*, man!" he exclaimed. "What happened to you?"

"It's a long story," Hugh answered as he limped forward.

"Come into my quarters," Brazeau said. "We have a noggin of brandy, while you tell me." Young Cayewa knew that Hugh had been wounded in that surprise attack of the Rees last summer, but he could easily see that something else had happened to him since then.

Beckoning Hugh on, he led the way into his living quarters, where a cheerful fire was burning in the wide fireplace. He sat Hugh down in a comfortable chair and poured his guest a generous glass of brandy.

Eager for the spirits, Hugh took a long swallow, then sputtered as he felt the fiery liquor warming his throat and insides. He took a more cautious sip and smacked his lips.

Brazeau was watching him intently, and Hugh realized that he was curious to hear his story. He had a friendly feeling for Young Cayewa. He was head of a rival fur company, but he was also an honest man. He'd always treated the men of the Rocky Mountain Fur Company fair and square.

Rivalry between the various fur companies was often intense as they competed with one another for furs and the favor of Indian tribes. But if a general Indian threat developed—as had happened with the Arikaras—they would quickly rally to one another's defense. And when individual members of rival companies met man-to-man, they were usually hospitable and friendly with one another.

Young Cayewa was such a man, Hugh reflected. Nevertheless, he had no intention of telling him the whole story of his abandonment. Instead, he related how he'd left Major Henry's group one day to hunt, only to be attacked and nearly killed by a grizzly. His companions had never found him, he said, but he'd survived. Now here he was. Listening to the story of the long crawl, Joseph Brazeau shook his head, half in amazement, half in sympathy.

"And now," Hugh concluded, "I'd like to get a good rifle and some balls and powder and a few other fixin's from the supplies Gen'ral Ashley left here, so's I can head on fer Henry's fort. I reckon he'd as lief I got what I need, seein' as I work fer 'im. I'll sign fer the lot."

Young Cayewa nodded in agreement. "Go over to the storehouse; my clerk show you where everything is," he answered. "And when you're ready, come back here. We'll eat and talk some more. *Oui*?"

Nightfall found Hugh wearing a new flannel shirt under the deerskin hunting jacket that Badger's wives had made for him. He also had new buckskin leggings, a pullover woolen cap, another pair of thick-soled moccasins, and a knee-length flannel cloak with a hood. Besides these articles of clothing, the clerk had issued him a new flintlock rifle, a powder horn and powder, a supply of bullets, and a new hunting knife, as well as a blanket, tin cup, pan, small kettle, and rations of tea, tobacco, and salt.

Hugh had also picked out a long length of red-and-blue calico and a supply of trade beads, tobacco, and vermilion. These he had promptly taken to Badger as gifts for his two wives and himself. This business attended to, he headed back to Young Cayewa's quarters. He hoped to be on his way to the Yellowstone right quick, he told Brazeau as they sat down to eat the evening meal.

"*Non, non, mon ami,*" Young Cayewa exclaimed. "You stay here, rest up a few days. It is a long way to Henry's fort, and soon it be cold—lots of snow." Hugh shook his head in reply. He wanted to head on, he said, "come hell or high water, or freezin' time."

After they had eaten, Brazeau bade Hugh take off his new jacket and shirt so he could treat the still raw wound on his back. "Those Sioux did a good job on you," he observed. After disinfecting the wound with alcohol, he added a soothing salve and carefully bandaged it.

"Now—you get a good night's sleep, and stay here a few days," he urged once more. "Soon it be cold . . . snow come . . . upper Missouri freeze. With that leg and back, you're not ready to take off for the Yellowstone."

Hugh was resolute. "I'll stay a couple of days," he said, "but then I reckon I'll be on my way. This child ain't gonna let a bit of winter stop him." He thumped his chest lightly. "Why, there's still leaves on some of the trees," he went on. "Still a while afore freezin' time sets in." He paused a moment to savor the brandy in front of him. "Your clerk says that you're aimin' to send a party upstream in two, three days with trade goods for the Mandans. How 'bout me goin' along on that little expedition? I c'n hunt fer the crew—and the boat will take me partway to the Yellowstone."

Brazeau shook his head in resignation. "Crazy man," he observed, "but if you must go, you must. *Oui*, you can go as far as the Mandans in my boat."

9

A Daring Rescue

Brazeau knew well that he was taking some risks in sending a trading mission to the Mandans that fall. It would be the first trading venture upriver since the recent campaign against the Rees, and there was no telling how it would be received. The Mandans had been stirred up a bit after the burning of the Arikara villages, he told Hugh, but they should be calmed down by now. After all, they had always been friendly to white men.

The Rees were the ones that Young Cayewa was worried about. As yet, no one really knew where they had gone after their defeat. Rumor had it that some of them had traveled southwest and joined their Pawnee relatives near the headwaters of the Platte. If so, good riddance, Young Cayewa commented. But for all he knew some of them might still be in the North Country. No telling how they would react if they met the trading mission.

"*C'est bon* if Rees do keep peace," Brazeau said with an expressive shrug. "We hope! But there be some risk, *n'est-ce pas?*"

Hugh nodded. "Jest 'bout everything a man ever faces poses some risk or other," he commented, "be it Indians, or beaver trappin', or huntin'. A little trip up the Missouri ain't no different."

The leader of the upcoming venture, Brazeau told him, would be Antoine Citoleaux, his second-in-command at Fort Kiowa. Known up and down the river by the nickname Langevin, the Frenchman had many years of experience on the Missouri and had always gotten along well with both Indians and white trappers.

Toussaint Charbonneau would be going along as an interpreter. He was an old hand on the Upper Missouri, too; in 1805 he and his Shoshone wife, Sacajawea, had accompanied Lewis and Clark on their pioneering journey up the Missouri and to the Pacific Coast. Hugh would be the hunter for the group, which would also include four boatmen to row.

Two days later the seven men left Fort Kiowa and headed upstream in a big mackinaw—a stout, flat-bottomed boat commonly used to transport loads of trade goods. It had a square sail that could be set when the winds were favorable, but at this time of year the members of the crew had to spend most of their time rowing.

Boatmen poling cargo bullboats, made of buffalo hides, on the North Platte River at Scotts Bluff. Note the Indian in the small, saucer-shaped bullboat at right.

Progress upriver was slow, even though the four boatmen pulled mightily with their oars. The current was strong, and they had to buck chill October winds sweeping down from the north. Hugh went ashore to hunt each evening, and his luck was good. The first day out he killed a white-tailed buck that he surprised when it came to the edge of a sandbar to drink. On the second day he bagged an antelope. He'd see to it that the crew ate well.

As for himself, what he wanted was to get to Henry's post on the Yellowstone as soon as possible. There he'd finally have it out with Fitzgerald and Bridger. The black anger still bubbled up within him at the very thought of those faithless two. And to think that he'd once considered them friends!

Langevin, the leader of the mission, was silent and moody most of the time. He was worried about this trip, he confided to Hugh. What if the Arikaras had come back to the Upper Missouri, as some claimed? What if the party encountered them on the way upriver?

"You can't trust them," he declared, and Hugh had to agree. The old bullet wound on his thigh bore witness to that. The treachery of the Rees was known to every mountain man on the frontier. Even if their chiefs wanted peace for a while, they'd be hard put to control their young warriors. If the mission met any Rees, they'd still be out for blood.

On they rowed, past sandbars and high bluffs, with silvered snags from the spring flood still lining the banks of the river. Here and there on the sandy banks Hugh noted beaver slides—not many of them, though, for most of the beaver had been trapped out this far south. Everywhere, the trees along the river were shedding their leaves. Golden rafts of them were constantly drifting past the boat.

From time to time they saw little bands of pronghorns or buffalo, and occasionally an elk or a deer at the water's edge. There was more meat about than they would ever need, Hugh reflected. Pity he'd gotten so little of it on his crawl, but that was because he had no weapons—and couldn't walk, besides. He touched with satisfaction the new flintlock rifle that Young Cayewa had issued to him. A man needed his rifle, his bullets, and his powder horn in this country. Not only to get food, but also to use against Indians if need be.

The farther north they pushed, the more depressed and worried Langevin became. He sat in the prow of the mackinaw most of the time, gazing ahead and brooding over what might happen next.

"*Cela va mal*," he told Hugh. "Things will go badly. I

feel it in my bones." He made the sign of the cross and sighed deeply. At Cedar Island, just a mile below the Teton River, he wrote out his last will and testament and left it with a couple of traders they met there. Hugh shook his head. For whatever reason, Langevin was feeling hexed.

On they went, past the muddy waters of the Teton River, past the Cheyenne and Moreau. Ah, Hugh thought, he knew these waters! The Grand was next. A few miles beyond the mouth of the river they passed the burned and deserted Ree villages. No signs of life anywhere, Hugh observed, except for a couple of mangy-looking Indian dogs that came down to the shore and howled as the boat passed.

November had come by this time, and the country was beginning to take on the look of approaching winter. No snow as yet, but the trees were bare and the prairie grasslands were brown and yellow. Every morning frost lay in silver patches on the ground. Most of the migrating birds were gone. Now they saw only the birds of winter—crows and magpies, the occasional hawk or eagle, the little flocking sparrows.

On they advanced into the barren, windswept country of the Upper Missouri. They passed through a brief snow shower near the mouth of the Cannonball River, and another when they came to the Heart River. Now, a week above the Grand, they were approaching the Mandan villages.

So far they hadn't seen any Indians at all, except for a few friendly Sioux during the first days of the trip. Langevin, however, remained worried and depressed. The farther north they went, the lower his spirits seemed to sink.

Hugh could see that Charbonneau was getting edgy, too. The day before they were due to arrive at the Mandan village, Charbonneau asked to be put ashore. He would walk cross-country to the Mandans, he said. He'd probably get there before the boat did.

The next day, when the mackinaw was just a few miles below the Mandan village, Hugh decided that he would go ashore to hunt at a place where the river started a big loop. He and Langevin had agreed that a gift of fresh meat might help to smooth their meeting with the Indians. He would walk across the neck of land between the sides of the loop, he told Langevin, and hope to bag a deer or an antelope by the time he met the boat again.

The boatmen steered the mackinaw into the sandy shore on the western side of the river, and Hugh climbed out. As the boat edged back into the main channel, Hugh headed for a patch of bushes where a little creek flowed

Mandan village overlooking the Missouri River, from a painting by Karl Bodmer. Bullboats, made by stretching buffalo hides over a wooden framework, are shown in the foreground.

into the river. Soon he was walking through a thick grove of cottonwoods and willows.

He hadn't gone more than a quarter of a mile when he heard the sound of musket fire from the river, mixed with loud war whoops and screams. Hugh swore under his breath. The mackinaw was under attack. Rees, sure as shooting! They'd ambushed the men in the boat—Langevin's fears had come true!

Keeping to the cover of the trees, Hugh backtracked as fast as he could. Maybe he could help his comrades drive the Indians away. Near the place where he'd left the boat he peered out from a thicket of trees. There, on the shore, was a band of twenty or more Ree warriors in full war regalia—red paint and feathers and hornlike headdresses. They were whooping and shouting as they danced about the beached mackinaw, and Hugh could see they were transferring all the trade goods into several pirogues. Of Langevin and the four crewmen of the mackinaw there was no sign. Then he saw a couple of the Rees gleefully holding up bloody scalps. His companions had been massacred, Hugh realized—every one of them.

Hugh crept back the way he had come, keeping to cover all the way, and headed as fast as he could toward the Mandan villages. From what he'd heard, they were located a few miles upstream. This was unfamiliar territory, and he had to go by instinct. Had to watch out for Rees, too.

He had gone two miles, he judged, and was just rounding a bend in the tiny stream he was following when he came upon two Arikara women digging roots. At the sight of him they turned and fled, screaming at the tops of their lungs. Ahead of them, not a quarter of a mile away, Hugh

Bird's-eye view of a Mandan village as seen by George Catlin. The bullboat on the roof of the nearest lodge was used to cover the smoke hole during heavy rains.

could see a number of dirt lodges. He had stumbled into an Arikara village! Even as he looked, several Ree warriors, alerted by the cries of the women, came running out of their lodges. When they spotted Hugh they yelled triumphantly and raced toward him, rifles and bows in hand.

Hugh still walked with a slight limp, but he retreated as fast as he could, dodging and ducking through the trees. In spite of his best efforts, however, the Arikara warriors gained rapidly on him. A couple of rifle shots whistled past, and he felt that his last hour had surely come. Now he could hear the Rees whooping behind him, in anticipation of lifting his scalp.

Interior of the lodge of a Mandan chief as depicted by Karl Bodmer. Several families often lived together in earth-covered dwellings like this. Prized horses were sometimes stabled in the lodge as well. Shields, spears, baskets, and other utensils hung from the poles. Note the buffalo headdress, used in ceremonial dances.

Suddenly, from the side, he saw two Indians on horseback galloping toward him. Dashing up beside him, the leading horseman held out his hand and beckoned Hugh to get up behind him. The second horseman positioned himself between them and the pursuing Rees. These mounted men, Hugh suddenly realized, were Mandans, not Rees.

Pulled up onto the horse's rump by his rescuer, he clung to the Mandan's waist for dear life as the horse galloped away, followed by the second. Soon the Rees were left far behind. All Hugh could hear was their frustrated cries of rage.

A few minutes later they arrived at the Mandan village, which was located no more than a mile above the Rees'. After they dismounted, the Indian who saved Hugh ushered him into a big, mounded earth lodge. The light inside was dim, with just a small fire flickering in the center, the smoke escaping from a small opening at the top. Various utensils and other equipment were hung from the sloping roof, and a number of women and children looked at Hugh with friendly but curious eyes. Several families evidently lived in this big lodge.

One of the elder men spoke to Hugh in halting English. He was Gray Owl, he said, the father of Painted Feather, the young man who had rescued him. The Mandans were very angry with the Arikaras, he said. When the Arikaras had settled near them, they had promised to keep the peace with the white men. But they had already broken their pledge several times—the latest being the attack on Hugh.

"That ain't all," Hugh told Gray Owl. "Them Rees really are bad medicine!" He went on to relate how the party of Arikara warriors had ambushed Langevin and the four crewmen of the trading mission not three hours before. "And for all I know, they got Charbonneau, too. He set out afoot fer yer village yesterday."

Charbonneau had come safely into the Mandan village just that morning, Gray Owl assured Hugh. His wrinkled old face was grim, as he considered this latest news. "Arikaras should leave Mandan country," he said at last. "Mandans should send them away."

Easier said than done, Hugh reflected. The only way to get rid of the Rees is to fight them away!

A few minutes later, Charbonneau entered the lodge and

greeted Hugh. When he heard what had happened to his comrades he shook his head sadly.

"You an' me—we be lucky ones," he said. "But—Langevin and others—*les pauvres hommes*! I think I stay with my friends the Mandans awhile, till things settle down. Then head back to Fort Kiowa."

"Not me," Hugh told him. "I'm goin' on to the Yellowstone, quick as I can."

After giving Hugh a meal of cornmeal mush and venison, Painted Feather and his father escorted him to Tilton's Fort, an outpost of the Columbia Fur Company, at the edge of their village.

It was a poor excuse for a fort, Hugh thought as he gazed at it. Really just a little blockhouse cabin, with narrow openings for rifles on the second floor. How could the traders survive with such feeble defenses?

William Tilton himself unbarred the door and let them in after he had first checked and identified them to his satisfaction through one of the rifle openings. He was a big bluff man with curly black hair, clean-shaven except for a bristly moustache.

"I had my fort over on the other side of the river until a couple of months ago," he explained to Hugh. "Then the Rees came up here. They killed one of my men some weeks ago, and the rest of us had to take refuge with the Mandans until we built this post." He shook his head. "Even so, the Rees laid siege to it until the Mandans sent them off. Now I have just three men with me, and we hardly dare go outside."

"Aye, the Rees are bad'ns!" Hugh observed. Gray Owl and Painted Feather nodded in agreement. Hugh then told

Bison dance of the Mandan Indians, by Karl Bodmer. In 1833, Bodmer and Prince Maximilian of Wied witnessed this dance when they visited the Mandans. Maximilian noted that "They wear the skin of the upper part of the head, the mane of the buffalo with its horns. . . . The men with the buffalo heads always keep in the dance at the outside of the group, imitate all the motions and sounds of this animal."

Tilton what had happened to him, as well as to Langevin and all his crew. He explained that he aimed to head on for the Yellowstone immediately.

"The Rees'll know afore morning that I'm here at your blockhouse," he said. "That'll do you no good—or me, neither. I aim to shove on tonight."

10

To the Mouth of the Yellowstone

After thinking about it for a moment, William Tilton slowly nodded in agreement. The Rees would find out soon enough that Hugh Glass was in his post. They would watch the blockhouse, waiting for Hugh to leave, then ambush him when he was out of sight of the Mandans. Better he be on his way this very night.

The two Mandans also agreed. "Arikara chiefs not able to control their young braves—the hotheads," Gray Owl asserted. He went on to tell how one band under the leadership of a vengeful Ree warrior had left when they heard of the peace pledge. Unwilling to agree to the terms, they had gone south, Gray Owl said, to join up with their relatives, the Wolf Pawnees.

"Now Mandans sorry we let Arikara settle here," Gray Owl concluded.

Hugh nodded in agreement. As far as he was concerned, the Rees were a bad lot—treacherous, untrustworthy, out to ambush whites whenever they could. But he'd fool them. He'd be out of here before they realized he'd gone.

Could Tilton spare him a few supplies? he asked. He had lost everything when the Rees attacked Langevin's mackinaw. Ashley would square accounts. Would his Mandan friends, Painted Feather and Gray Owl, give him some rations for the journey, and would they ferry him across the river under cover of darkness so he could head for the Yellowstone on the left bank? Less chance of running into Rees over there. They all could and would.

A few hours later, he was on his way. Between the friendly Mandans and William Tilton of the Columbia Fur Company, he was as ready for the winter journey to the Yellowstone as he ever would be.

Tilton had replenished his bullet and powder supply and given him a ration of salt and tea, as well as a warm blanket and a small iron kettle. The Mandans had given him an extra pair of moccasins and a couple of leather bags filled with pemmican. Pemmican would last indefinitely, and a little of it would go a long way to keep a body moving. In addition to all this, he had the rifle, small ax, and knife he had picked up at Fort Kiowa six weeks before. He had his leather leggings and the warm knee-length flannel cloak, as well.

With his blanket, pot, and other supplies in a backpack,

Hugh followed Painted Feather and another young Mandan down to the sandy shore of the Missouri just before midnight.

The two Indians pushed into the river a small pirogue that had been drawn up on the bank, and motioned to Hugh to get in. The small canoe teetered precariously as he settled himself in the center section while the Indians took their places fore and aft. In the rear position, Painted Feather shoved the canoe off.

Hugh could feel a cold wind sweeping down from the North Country. He could hear the quiet gurgle of the current as the Indians dug their paddles into the water, taking them toward the opposite shore. The night was dark, for there was no moon, and only a few stars glimmered through a cover of clouds. Hugh was sure that the Rees had not noted their departure.

Finally he could make out the darker bulk of the east bank rising up before them. In a few moments he felt the pirogue scrape bottom as it came in to the sandy shore. Getting out, Hugh thanked his Indian helpers. He shook their hands, then watched while the canoe headed back across the dark waters.

There were good Indians like these, he reflected, and there were bad ones, too. Just like any other kind of *hombres.* You couldn't find better men than General Ashley or Major Henry, for instance. But there were worthless skunks like John Fitzgerald and Jim Bridger, too. Waugh! He'd once thought that the young 'un had better stuff in him. Well, he'd soon teach both him and Fitz that they couldn't desert a *compañero* without paying for it.

Pack on his back, rifle in hand, Hugh groped his way

through the dead stubs of driftwood along the bank, then with some difficulty swung himself up onto the higher land above the bluffs. Pausing to catch his breath, he looked about for possible danger. He could see better now, for some of the clouds had lifted. Ahead were patches of trees, mostly a thicket of small cottonwoods overlaid with grapevines. The night had become very cold, and he could feel the sting of snow flurries against his face. Aie! Winter was almost on him, and it was three hundred miles to Henry's post at the mouth of the Yellowstone—three hundred miles of cold country with the chance that Rees were on his trail. There was the chance also of running into Minatarees or Assiniboines, too—or Blackfeet, worst of all. The first two were sometimes friendly to trappers, sometimes not. But the Blackfeet made no bones about their hatred of whites.

As he tramped northward along the Missouri's left bank, the sky cleared entirely and more and more stars appeared overhead. Good. Now he had no trouble at all in seeing what was about him. He pushed on, as fast as he could go, but his progress was slow. Even though his wounds were all healing, he still felt the effects of that fight with the old she-grizzly. He'd abandoned the crutch by now, but carried a stout cane instead. It would be some time before he got all his strength back.

By dawn, he'd done nearly a dozen miles, he reckoned. Shivering, he made his way into a little grove of willows near the bluff looking over the river. After eating a few mouthfuls of pemmican, he rolled up in his blanket and slept the sleep of the exhausted.

When he woke in late afternoon, he had another meal of pemmican, then headed on, his rifle loaded and ready for Indians or for meat on the hoof, if either came into sight. It wasn't until late the next day, however, that he surprised a young doe mule deer as she came down to the river's edge to drink. He killed her with a single shot, then quickly hid himself in a nearby thicket of brush and waited to find out whether the sound of his shot would bring any Indians to investigate. A half hour went by. Nothing. Then he spotted a couple of coyotes coming from the prairie toward the deer carcass. They'd evidently gotten the scent of fresh blood. Rising, he scared off the coyotes, then quickly skinned his quarry and cut off some of the choice pieces of venison—as much, he figured, as he could conveniently carry.

Leaving the rest to the coyotes that sat quietly waiting, he went on into a thick stand of cedar and brushy willows. He started a small fire in a sheltered spot with his flint and steel, and soon had fresh venison roasting over the nearly smokeless flame. He licked his lips in anticipation as he smelled the roasting meat. Unable to wait, he tore off a full mouthful of the sizzling flesh and gulped it down. Ah, but it was good! After that, he fell to and gorged on venison until he could eat no more. Satisfied at last, he cut a portion of the remaining meat into thin strips which he hung over the fire to cure a bit. It would keep longer that way. After packing the meat into one of his bags, he settled down to sleep.

Day after day he traveled doggedly onward. He was in snow country now. Several times he was buffeted by freezing sleet or snow and had to trudge through drifts, some of them nearly a foot deep. I should make myself some snowshoes, he told himself. As soon as he'd said it, though, he'd push into an area where the wind had swept the snow away—bare ground beneath his feet. Still, it was slow going, for he was not yet his old self. As much as anything, his will and determination kept him going—that, and his thoughts of revenge.

It would take him at least two weeks, he figured, to get from the Mandan village to the Yellowstone, if he averaged twenty miles a day. Of course that would depend on the weather—and the Indians. He'd been lucky so far—no signs of any. The weather was too cold for them, he thought. They'd be keeping close to their fires and the warmth of their lodges. The weather was cold, no question about it. But if it kept the Indians at home and let him travel in peace, that was fine by him.

It was early December when Hugh trudged to the top of a snowy rise and first spied the broad mouth of the Yellowstone several miles ahead, sweeping into the Missouri from the south. What's more, there in the tongue of land between the two rivers he could see the palisades of Henry's post.

Darkness was descending by the time Hugh reached the place where he could look directly at Fort Henry from the other side of the Missouri. It had taken him fifteen exhausting days to get here from Fort Tilton, he reflected—and he felt as if he was about at the end of his tether. The light was fading fast, and he couldn't detect any signs of life about the fort—no lights, no movement, no sounds. He shrugged his shoulders. Tomorrow would be soon enough to find out what was going on. But first, he'd have to get himself across to the other side of the river. Finding a sheltered spot in a gully, he wrapped himself in his blanket and slept.

Up at dawn the next morning, he noted that ice was

beginning to form along the shores of the river, edging out from the driftwood and stubs of dead cottonwoods uprooted by spring floods of the past. After eating a cold breakfast, he made his way some distance upstream of the fort. Time now to make himself a makeshift raft good enough to get him across the river.

After a search, he found two cottonwood logs, each about a foot in diameter and eight feet long. Trimming off the branches, he rolled the two logs onto the sandy shore and positioned them side by side. After another search, he found enough tough grapevine to bind the logs together. Nothing much to look at, he thought as he gazed at his crude raft, but it should hold together long enough to get him across the river. Finally, he shaped a flat piece of deadwood into a paddle with his ax and knife. He was all set to go.

After binding his rifle and all his gear to his back, he waded out beyond the driftwood and the icy banks of the Missouri, pulling his raft with him. When the water was thigh deep, he scrambled aboard and set out for the opposite shore, paddling strongly. He was a mile upstream from Fort Henry—far enough, he figured, to get him across to the fort before the current swept him past the mouth of the Yellowstone.

He'd calculated right, he discovered, but without much leeway. The current was stronger than he'd thought. He edged ashore just a few hundred yards before the Yellowstone swept into the mighty Missouri. Abandoning his log raft, he headed for the fort, his rifle at the ready. Still no sign of life.

When he got close enough, he saw that the big main

gate of the fort was open. Halting in a coulee, he watched the entrance for many minutes before he was sure that no one was there. What had happened to Major Henry and his *compañeros*? he wondered. Had the Blackfeet gotten them all?

Advancing cautiously, he entered the fort and walked into several cabins. All were empty, nothing left behind except a few wooden chairs and tables and random heaps of trash. No sign of a struggle, either. Major Henry and the others had evidently just lit out. But where had they gone?

He made a circuit of the entire inside of the fort, wanting to be certain he hadn't missed anything. When he left the stockade, he started a similar walk around the outside, searching for clues. Almost immediately he saw a flat slab of wood nailed to the stockade on one side of the big gate. On it someone had burnt a huge arrow, pointing south along the course of the Yellowstone.

11

New Year's Eve at Fort Henry

Hugh gazed in the direction indicated by the arrow. There flowed the Yellowstone. The message was clear. Major Henry and all his men—Jim Bridger and John Fitzgerald among them—had abandoned this post at the junction of the Yellowstone and Missouri and headed upriver. Maybe they figured the beaver trapping would be better upstream. Or maybe the Blackfeet had made things too hot for them here, and they had headed on for the country of the friendly Crow Indians. Whatever the reason—they were gone.

Hugh let out a grunt of exasperation, then sighed deeply.

To push so hard, to come so far, and then find—nothing. Feeling completely let down and frustrated, he gazed resentfully at the open gate, then drove his fist against his thigh. Waugh! Almost too hard to endure. Then he felt a new surge of determination rise up within him. Well, he too would head on, he told himself. He'd find them sooner or later!

His mind made up, he didn't wait. There was nothing of any use to him here, and he'd better get going before any stray Blackfeet came by and found him. A wonder they hadn't already burned the deserted post.

He made only a few miles that day, for the weather was bitterly cold. A constant, bone-chilling wind blew down from Canada, and the snow was drifted deep in many areas. Hard going, especially for a body still recovering from a near-fatal bout with an old she-grizzly. By midafternoon the light was already beginning to fade, for in mid-December days were short in this northwest wilderness. Snowflakes whirled about him. High time to find some sheltered spot and hunker down for the night.

A short distance ahead, Hugh saw a deep gully, fringed by a growth of small trees and bushes. A frozen stream, no more than a few feet wide, meandered down from the rolling plains. The gully and trees, even without leaves, would give him some shelter from the wind.

Searching out a likely spot, he gathered dried twigs and driftwood and soon had a small fire started. He then filled his pot with snow, which he melted over the fire. Cutting up the last of his meat, he tossed the pieces into the bubbling pot and added the few frozen wild turnips he still had. When the stew was thick and steaming, he gulped it

American elk, or wapiti, chased by wolves.

down. Finished, he patted his stomach contentedly and sighed, then curled up in his blanket and settled himself to sleep. His last thought before he drifted off was of food. Tomorrow he must get some more meat.

Dawn was just beginning to lighten the horizon when Hugh was awakened by a chorus of excited wolf howls and the sound of splashing in the creek. Groping for his rifle, he staggered to his feet just in time to see a big old bull elk in the creek bed a hundred yards away. It had broken through the ice and was starting to clamber ashore. Behind it were six or seven wolves in close pursuit. Turning to face its tormentors, the elk scooped up one of the wolves in its antlers and tossed it into the creek. Then, before Hugh could get off a good shot at it, it had turned and fled, with the wolf pack chasing after it. In less than a minute their sounds were faint in the distance.

Fully awake by now, Hugh saw that the snowfall had stopped. The chill winds were still blowing, however, and the cold was more bitter than ever. From time to time he heard cracking noises as frozen limbs of cottonwoods or willows splintered and broke. After swallowing a few mouthfuls of pemmican, Hugh plodded onward through the snow, ever on the lookout for signs of men—either trappers or Indians—and ever on the lookout for game.

As he took a shortcut between two bends in the river, he crossed the open plains. Here the wind had piled the snow in deep drifts in some places and had swept the land almost bare in others. He crossed the frozen ice of a small stream and saw the snowcapped dome of a large beaver lodge ahead of him. Aie! If he could get into that lodge and snag a fat beaver, he could have a feast. But no chance of that, he told himself. First blow of his ax on the lodge and the beaver'd be gone.

Skirting the tree-fringed banks of the frozen stream, he saw a crow and two magpies fly up. They must have been feeding on something. Tramping over to investigate, he found the bones and ragged skin of a white hare. There was no meat left, though. The birds had picked the carcass clean.

As he trudged on, he took out another handful of pemmican and gnawed on it. Only a bit of it left. He had to get some other food. And luck was with him. Near dusk he surprised a coyote with its fresh kill—another white hare. Taking quick aim, Hugh shot the wild dog, killing it. Had to risk the sound of the shot, he told himself. He immediately reloaded his rifle and waited in concealment for some minutes, in case any Indians came to investigate.

Finally satisfied, he approached the coyote cautiously. It was dead, all right. And the hare was a big one. The coyote hadn't even started to eat it.

"Sorry, my friend," he said to the coyote. "You were hungry, and I was, too. Thanks for helping me out—even though you didn't mean to."

It was already midafternoon. The wind had strengthened, promising another frigid night. Soon it would be dark, Hugh thought. Might as well make a camp here—as good a place as any. Finding a sheltering bank, he piled up dead driftwood to form a sort of lean-to, then laid smaller branches across the top. That done, he made a small fire and began to skin his quarry—the rabbit first, then the coyote. Soon his pot was bubbling with rabbit stew. After eating, he cut thin strips of the coyote meat and cured them slightly over the fire. He'd carry enough to hold him over for a few days. Smoked and frozen, the meat would keep.

As he curled up for sleep that night he heard wolves howling in the distance. The wind moaned through the branches of the willows above him. The fire burned low, giving little heat. Stars glowed in the clear sky, and he saw a moving shadow on the snow as a big white owl glided low over the rim of the windswept plains. An Arctic ghost owl, he observed. At least that's what he called it. The owl was hungry, too. Best of luck, he thought, as he fell asleep.

Day after day went by as Hugh made his way up the Yellowstone River. Past what must be the Powder and Tongue rivers, past a creek he'd heard Major Henry call the Rosebud. The frozen land was covered deep with snow, and the going was slow, even when he wore the crude snowshoes he'd finally made for himself, using frozen willow branches which he'd heated and shaped for the frames, and strips of the coyote's hide for webbing. Sometimes he made a dozen or fifteen miles a day, sometimes less. He was always so tired and footsore by midafternoon that he scarcely had strength to make camp and prepare his supper.

Where in tarnation had Major Henry and his men built their new fort, anyhow? Hugh wondered. He'd been on the way from the mouth of the Yellowstone for nigh onto two weeks. No sign of Indians, no sign of his old companions, no sign of beaver trappers anywhere. So far, he'd survived because of the coyote meat he'd taken way back—that and a couple of rabbits he'd surprised. Slim fare, but he was used to little. He would manage.

One afternoon, however, he felt that something new in weather was coming his way. It had been cold enough so far, what with frigid winds and snowdrifts, and here and there a brisk snowfall. Nothing too bad. But this afternoon had a feeling of something more. The wind was moaning through the trees and great limbs were cracking and falling. The sky was overcast; by early afternoon it was almost dark. Only a strange pale yellow light showed where the sun hung low in the western sky. Snow was beginning to fall—big white flakes that swirled about him, driven by the wind. Time to find shelter, he told himself as the wind quickened. Night seemed only minutes away.

Soon the snowfall became so heavy that he couldn't see more than a few feet ahead of him. One thing about such weather, he told himself with a wry smile—no Indians would be out in it.

Stumbling into a small creek bottom, he found a ledge of rock that seemed to afford shelter. Exhausted, he crawled into the shallow cave formed by the overhanging rock. After eating a few mouthfuls of dried coyote meat, he curled up in his blanket. In a few minutes he was asleep.

When he wakened he didn't know what time it was, or even whether it was night or day. The opening of the ledge was covered over with snow—snow that had swept down from the plains above and drifted over most of the entrance. Waugh! A midwinter blizzard—that's what he was in now. He investigated the one small opening still left in his cave. It was dim daylight outside, with the wind whistling and heavy snow still falling. Well, he was in a snug shelter and had enough food to last several days, if he rationed it. Snuggling back into his blanket, he dozed off.

He remained in his snow tepee for three days while the storm swirled over him, blanketing the high plains with a thick white mantle that the wind drifted many feet thick in some areas. Hugh kept a small chimney hole open and was able to keep reasonably warm, especially when he nursed a small fire fed with pieces of dead wood he found at one end of his natural shelter. He ate the meat of the coyote, brewed hot tea from the supply Tilton had given him, slept, and thought about what lay ahead.

The new Fort Henry couldn't be too far away. And when he got there, he'd find Jim Bridger and John Fitzgerald. His heart leaped in bitter anticipation at the thought. The will to find those two had been the force that had driven him ever since the Grand; he was determined to give them their just deserts—those two who had left him to die.

In many ways this enforced rest was a good thing, he told himself. He'd been pushing at a pretty hard pace, and his old bones ached.

At last the storm abated and he was able to dig himself out of his hideaway and set out on his journey once again. By now, he figured, it must be close to the end of the year. The air was as cold as ever, but a bright sun shone high in the sky, making the snow a glare of shining whiteness everywhere he looked. Had to be careful not to go snow blind, he told himself, closing his eyes to slits as he forged ahead.

The crust was glazed enough to bear Hugh's weight in most places, but in others he sank into the snow, making the going harder than ever. Stopping to put on his snowshoes, he trudged doggedly onward. He had been on his way for only a couple of hours when he heard sounds in a draw ahead of him. Pushing on, rifle at the ready, he saw an old buffalo cow in the distance, surrounded by wolves. She was sunk in the snow up to her flanks, and the big wild dogs circled about, each in turn dashing in to bite at her or fasten its teeth in her flanks. Bloody froth bubbled out of the embattled cow's nostrils as she struggled vainly to face and gore her tormentors, and the ground around her was stained with red. As Hugh approached, the wolves snarled and retreated.

Taking a steady aim, Hugh put the cow out of her misery. Then he opened her up and took as much meat as he could carry. This should hold him for another few days. Leaving the rest of the carcass to the wolves, he went on. It had been twenty-three days since he'd headed down the Yellowstone. If he didn't find his *compañeros* soon, he'd be out of luck—stuck in the northwest winter with nothing except a few wild beasts.

The next day he found a new sign—another big arrow burned into a piece of white driftwood and placed in the crotch of a dead tree where anybody coming along would be bound to see it. The arrow pointed across the frozen Yellowstone toward what Hugh thought must be the mouth of the Bighorn River, on the other side.

Hugh grimaced. Still a spell to go. But he had a feeling it couldn't be far now. Walking across the frozen river, he found another arrow, pointing directly up the Bighorn.

It was late afternoon two days later when he finally came in sight of his goal, no more than half a mile away—a new Fort Henry, built where the Little Bighorn River flowed into the Bighorn. His heart quickened at the sight of the high cottonwood and cedar stockade, the two blockhouses, the blue smoke from several fires curling above the walls.

Hastening on, he soon reached the main gate of the fort. It was closed, with not a sentry in sight. He could hear sounds coming from inside, however. Strange sounds. He listened, unbelieving. Someone was playing a lively tune on a fiddle—"Yankee Doodle." With hardly a stop the music switched to a sailor's hornpipe. Hugh could hear loud shouts, coarse singing, stomping feet. They were dancing a jig! What in thunder was going on?

Then the fiddle started another song—slow, familiar, throbbingly sweet: "Auld Lang Syne."

Should auld acquaintance be forgot,
and never brought to mind?
We've wandered mony a weary foot
sin Auld Lang Syne.
For Auld Lang Syne, my dear,
for Auld Lang Syne,
We'll take a cup of kindness yet,
for Auld Lang Syne.

As the last notes died out, Hugh heard loud laughter and more shouting. Then a single voice sounded out. "To the New Year! A toast to 1824! May it bring more beaver, fewer unfriendly Indians, fortunes for us all!" More cheers and shouts.

Hugh smiled grimly. So the boys were celebrating the coming of the New Year! He shook his head slowly, remembering the last time he'd heard that song, when his mother and father had sung it on New Year's Eve that first winter in the cabin on the Monongahela. Seems like a thousand years ago, he reflected. Abruptly, he shut off that memory and strode up to the gate.

"Open up in there, *compañeros,*" he bellowed. He gave a loud halloo and kicked impatiently at the door. "It's me—Glass—back from where you all left me," he continued as loud as he could shout. He waited a moment, then hammered at the gate once again.

After several minutes a head popped up from the sentry walk. Hugh saw that it was Hiram Allen. Hiram stared at Hugh and blinked. "Hugh Glass?" he stammered. "B-b-but you're dead!"

"Think so?" Hugh rasped. "Well, those two worthless critters that was left with me thought I'd be dead, too. But I ain't. Come on down and let this old hoss in. Pinch me, see that I ain't a ghost. Then you c'n get back to celebratin'."

It took only a moment for Hiram to come down and open the gate. He looked at Hugh as if he was indeed a ghost standing before him. Timidly he touched Hugh's arm and peered closely at his face, where the scars left by the bear were still vivid on his cheeks and forehead.

By this time several others had come to peer at the apparition and voice their wonder. Then Ned Appleby clapped him on the back. "We all figgered you was a goner!" he exclaimed. "How'd you get here?"

Hugh saw a tall figure come across the way. Major Henry. Approaching, the major stared at Hugh, as astonished as the others. He noted how thin and ragged Hugh was, how close to exhaustion he appeared to be.

"I don't believe it, Hugh!" he exclaimed at last. "All of us thought you long dead and gone. But here you are—

and welcome!" He gripped Hugh's shoulder companionably and shook his hand. "Come into my cabin," he went on. "We'll get you something to eat. Then I'd sure like to hear what happened to you."

Hugh held back, his rifle in the crook of his arm, ready. "I'm right glad to be here, Major," he declared. "But afore I tell you my story and have a bit to eat and drink, I've got some business to attend to. Where are those good-fer-nothin's, Fitzgerald and Bridger?"

A sudden silence fell over the group. Then the major spoke. "Fitzgerald's left us," he said. "Started downriver some six weeks ago. Figgered he wasn't cut out to be a trapper, I guess. If you came to us by way of the Missouri, you must have passed him on the way."

Hugh felt a stab of bitter disappointment. So John Fitzgerald had pushed on. "I'll find him," he muttered. Then, "What about Bridger?" he inquired.

"Jim's here," Major Henry responded, "but at the moment he's out hunting some meat for the mess."

At that moment someone shouted from outside the gate, and the sentry swung it open. There, standing in the entrance with a yearling mule deer slung across his broad shoulders, was young Jim.

When he saw Hugh, he stopped short and stared at him wide-eyed, the color slowly draining from his face. His expression reflected many conflicting emotions—astonishment, awe, joy, and horror—as he gazed at this specter from the past, the man he had left for dead.

12
Confrontation with Jim Bridger

The two men stood motionless for a long moment, staring at one another. Neither of them uttered a word.

Before him, Hugh saw the youth he had once thought of as a friend, who'd been left to look out for him the day after the grizzly fight. Bridger had filled out a bit since fall, Hugh noted, but his cheeks were still almost downy, and his Adam's apple was as prominent as ever. Right now it was bobbing up and down. Hugh watched with satisfaction as the boyish face paled.

"Hugh! Hugh Glass!" Jim finally blurted out. "Are you really . . . alive?"

"No thanks to you, ye worthless pup!" Hugh said. He felt his anger mounting as he continued to gaze at the younger man. "Speak up, Jim, afore I kills ye," he thundered at the boy. "Why did ye act the coward? Why did ye take my rifle and all my fixin's and leave me fer the wolves or Indians to finish off?" He started to raise his rifle. "You got anythin' to say fer yourself?"

Major Henry quickly stepped forward and pushed Hugh's rifle down. "There'll be no shooting here," he stated firmly. "Suppose you simmer down, Hugh, and come into my quarters with Jim. We'll talk. As I said, I want to hear your story."

"And I want to hear Jim's," Hugh said vehemently. Surprisingly, the violent anger within him seemed to be cooling a bit.The sight of that raw young 'un paling and in shock had done something. That and the song "Auld Lang Syne" that the fiddler had been playing as he approached the fort.

"I'll keep my rifle," he told Andrew Henry, "but I won't use it—inside the fort, anyway." He scowled at Jim. "I'm hankerin' to hear what this young pup has to say!"

The rest of the men watched silently as Major Henry led the way to his quarters, followed closely by Hugh, with Jim in the rear. Standing in front of the fireplace, where a warm fire crackled, the major poured stiff portions of brandy for all three of them.

While he and Hugh took chairs before the fire, the younger mountain man walked over to a bench in the corner of the room. There he hunched down, a picture of abject misery. Since his first startled outburst, he hadn't uttered a word. Silent and dejected, he was deathly pale. Serves him right, Hugh thought to himself. He should feel guilty. He had it coming. But in spite of himself, Hugh felt a twinge of pity for the boy.

"Hugh," Major Henry finally said after glancing at Jim, "we all thought you were dead and buried. I didn't even think you'd last the night after that grizzly bear was done with you there on the Grand. But here ye be. Tell me what happened."

"All in good time," Hugh answered gruffly. He pointed at Jim. "Let him tell his story first. You left him and Fitz with me. They was supposed to wait and bury me after I'd gone under. Oh, I know, he came back to join ye, pretty as ye please, no doubt sayin' that poor Old Hugh had died, and that they'd buried me right and proper before leavin'. That's what they told ye, isn't it?" he demanded. "Now let's hear the cowardly little coyote tell you what really happened. Let's hear him. Then I'll tell you what happened to me."

Major Henry looked over at Jim. "Fair enough," he said. "First, though, I'll tell you that young Jim has earned his keep here with us this winter. He's skirmished with the Blackfeet, along with the rest of us. He's worked steady at his trapping, got more beaver plews than most of the others. He's a good hunter and turning out to be a good mountain man."

He paused, then addressed himself directly to Jim. "Right now," he said, "I want to hear the real story of what happened after we left you last fall. Fitz isn't here to answer, but you are."

Jim looked up, his face agonized, his eyes full of pain as he noted Hugh's scarred face and throat. The older man looked scornfully back at him.

"Hugh!" Jim uttered, his voice breaking. He still seemed almost in a state of shock. "Hugh, I sure never expected to see ye alive again, but —but, I'm glad ye are!" he finished with a rush. "I'm glad—even iffen ye do kill me fer what I done. I deserve it, I guess."

"Ye shore do!" Hugh snarled at the youth. "You 'n' Fitz took my rifle and all my fixin's, then deserted me. I wouldn't a' done that to a dog. And don't fear, you're gonna pay fer it." He made as if to raise his rifle again, and Major Henry quickly restrained him.

"None of that!" he ordered. "Jim, get on with your story."

Jim gulped once and took a deep breath. Hugh could see him grit his teeth as he exhaled.

"It's just as Hugh said," he finally replied. "Fitz and I did our best fer him fer nigh onto five days. There was Indian sign, and we . . ." he hesitated and gulped, "we . . . took Hugh's gear and lit out."

"I left Fitz in charge," Major Henry observed. "Did he, perhaps, decide to abandon Hugh, and make you go along with that decision?"

"No," Jim blurted out miserably. "I ain't a'gonna excuse myself by blamin' Fitz. Iffen I'd had the gumption, I'd a' stayed by myself. What I done was wrong—I felt it then, and I know it now. I've knowed it ever since we left ye, Hugh, and many's the night I've laid awake, tryin' to sleep, but tormented by what we done by leavin' ye."

Hugh watched him intently, but said nothing.

"Thing is," Jim continued, "every mornin' we thought you was about dead, but ye hung on and hung on. Sometimes I thought ye was sure enough dead, but then ye'd give out a bit of a moan. Sometimes I couldn't even see ye breathin', figgered it was time to dig the grave fer ye."

Jim stumbled on, telling how they'd seen Indian signs, how they could hardly tell from one hour to the next whether Hugh was alive or dead. As he listened, Hugh felt more of his anger subside. He remembered dimly how Fitz had had a time persuading Jim to leave. Aye—he'd been drifting in and out of consciousness, but he'd heard enough to know what was what. Fitz had done the persuading—he was the more experienced and by far the older. He was more to blame than Jim. Maybe let this young 'un off, he began to think. That's what my Quaker grandmum would say.

". . . and that's what we done," Jim finally concluded, still gazing at Hugh. "Signs of Ree all about us, an' we figgered ye couldn't last more'n an hour or two, anyway. If we'd stayed, they'd probably've found us and scalped us all. So we took yer gear and headed out to join up with the others." He stopped for a moment.

"We done it, yes," he continued. "And I ain't proud of it. I know we done wrong. So iffen ye wanta shoot me fer it, Hugh, I can't hardly blame ye."

Hugh gazed at the youthful face, now flushed and downcast. He'd been fond of this boy—and Jim wasn't a full-grown man yet. He had good stuff in him once, he thought. Maybe he still did.

Suddenly Hugh made up his mind. "Young 'un," he finally said, "ye deserted me as ye said, and ye robbed me of my rifle and knife and everything else I needed. Ye left me fer dead—and I mostways was, as ye say. Iffen I had died, there'd a' been no one there to close my eyes or bury me and cover my grave with rocks so's the wolves wouldn't get my stringy old meat.

"But I didn't die. When I realized ye was gone—takin' everything of mine that might of helped me survive—I swore I'd track ye and Fitz down. I swore an oath on it that I'd come after the two of ye and give ye yer just deserts. Tit fer tat's fair play.

"I've made a long journey to get me here. But now, lookin' at ye, I can't do ye no harm. I see's y're sorry, and I won't kill ye. I forgive ye, Jim. But keep in mind what ye did to me. Never do it to another man."

At that, Jim got up, his face again white as a sheet, his Adam's apple working up and down as his eyes blurred with tears. Hugh and Major Henry watched silently as the youth walked slowly over to the door and went out.

Major Henry refilled Hugh's cup and took a bit more himself.

"You won't regret that, Hugh," he said quietly. "This experience, I'm thinking, will make Jim a better man in the long run. He has a lot of the right stuff in him."

"All to the good," Hugh answered. "I hope the young 'un does shape up, as ye say. But me forgivin' him doesn't mean I'm about to give up on gettin' Fitzgerald."

13
The Pursuit of Fitzgerald

Once the confrontation with Jim Bridger was over, Hugh felt more at ease than he had in a long time. That young 'un had made a mistake, but maybe he'd learned something from it for the long run. Yes, he felt good about forgiving Jim.

That didn't mean he'd forgive Fitzgerald, though. Whenever he thought of the other man, he felt the old resentment boiling up as bitter as ever. Aie! That one really should've known better. Hugh was still grimly determined to track him down. When he found him, he'd shoot him on sight. Fitz had it coming.

January, the moon of many cold nights, had settled in, with bitter Arctic winds constantly sweeping down from the Canadian plains. Time enough to go after Fitz when it got a bit warmer, Hugh told himself. Meanwhile, he'd go back to being one of the company, as Major Henry had suggested. Go trapping when the weather allowed, get a few beaver plews, do some hunting for the mess cooks.

He settled easily into the winter life of the fort, hunting and trapping with his old companions, swapping stories with them around a cabin fireplace in the evenings.

In such close quarters he and young Jim were bound to rub shoulders a bit. Hugh sensed that the old easy feeling between them was gone, replaced by a mutual strain and reserve. Things would never be the same. Whenever they passed each other, Jim would have a stricken look as their eyes met. Then he'd hurry on after a muttered greeting, his face flushed.

Jim was still feeling guilt, Hugh observed. That was all right. He shouldn't forget what he'd done. But he himself never again mentioned the desertion to Jim. He'd had his say that first night at Fort Henry. As for all the others, they accepted the fact that Hugh had forgiven young Bridger. Since he had, why should they hold the incident against him? Bridger was one of them, and they all liked him.

As the weeks went by, Hugh hunted and trapped, ate three square meals a day, and slept in a comfortable bunk in a warm cabin. His wounds had all healed by now. He would carry the scars for the rest of his life, and, after that big grizzly had nearly torn his throat out, his voice would never be the same. But he felt in good shape again at last.

He might be more than twice the age of most of the others, he told himself, but he could hold his own with any of them.

January gave way to February, and the days were a bit longer, but as bitterly cold as ever. Late in the month warm chinook winds blew eastward from the distant Rockies, bringing a spell of mild weather. Hugh began to get itchy feet. About time to be on his way, he thought, time to hunt Fitzgerald down and settle with him.

Major Henry didn't know where Fitz had gone, but

Mountain men setting traps for beaver. The trap, attached by a chain to a stick driven into or near the bank, is hidden underwater. A small branch baited with castor, an oily substance obtained from beaver glands, is positioned immediately over the trap. A "float stick" is attached to the trap so that if the trapped beaver carries it away, the stick will point out its position. The painting is by Alfred Jacob Miller.

several of the mountain men told Hugh that he'd evidently had a bellyful of life in the wilderness, with the constant threat of losing his scalp to a Blackfoot or some other Indian every time he went out to set his beaver traps. One of the company, Cyrus Field, said that Fitz had let drop he was going to head down to Fort Atkinson and join the Army. That would be the place to look for him, Hugh told himself.

When Major Henry let it be known one day that he had some dispatches and letters that he wanted taken down to Fort Atkinson for posting to General Ashley in St. Louis, Hugh went to see him immediately.

"Trappin' season's 'bout over, Major," he said, "and I'd just as soon carry yer letters down to the fort. Seems like I'm not the body t'stay in any one place fer long, and I'm hankerin' to be on the move again. You can be certain I'll get them letters of yours wherever you want 'em."

"It's a long trip, Hugh," Major Henry said. "And no telling what the Indians might be doing along the way. You sure you're up to it?"

Hugh drew himself up and stared levelly at Andrew Henry. "I was up to crawlin' from the Grand to Fort Kiowa," he thundered, "then upriver in midwinter, and findin' ye after ye moved here to the Little Bighorn. Gettin' to Fort Atkinson'll be no problem."

"Point taken," Major Henry replied, smiling. "All right, Hugh. You're the man to take my messages to Fort Atkinson. Seeing as it's a long trip, however, and all through Indian country, I'm sending four other men with you. Five can do better than one man on his own if an emergency comes up."

Hugh felt differently—he'd made it from the Mandan

village to the Bighorn on his own in dead of winter, hadn't he? But he didn't argue. The four men to go with him were Ken Marsh and Dave More, two young mountain men who'd come from Indiana in the first place; Luke Chapman, a taciturn Missouri farmer who'd been in the fur trading business for the past two seasons; and Dan Dutton, an experienced trapper from Nebraska. It was early March when the five of them set out.

As they passed through the gate, Hugh glanced back for one last look at Fort Henry. There was young Bridger near his cabin, watching them go. Bridger hesitated as his eyes met Hugh's; then he half raised his hand in a farewell. Hugh gazed at the young man for a long moment, then raised his hand in a short answering salute. Turning quickly, he trudged off across the snowy plains with the others.

Instead of heading out by way of the Yellowstone and Missouri Rivers, which were largely frozen over, the five men headed cross-country, going southeast across Rosebud Creek and the headwaters of the Tongue until they hit the valley of the Powder River. Then, traveling as fast as they could, they headed southward through the valley of the Powder until they hit its headwaters. From there they pushed overland almost straight south toward the upper reaches of the North Platte River.

Until now they had been in rugged hill country, the range of shining mountains to the west covered with snow that glowed pink in the rays of the morning sun. One night, bedded down in his blankets, Hugh looked up at the stars looming overhead. A crescent moon climbed the eastern sky, and he saw the Big Dipper pointing to the North Star.

Strange lights, the glow of the Arctic, flickered and shimmered above the hills—streamers of red, pale green, blue, and yellow.

A place to live and hunt—and die, Hugh thought to himself as he gazed upward. Would be perfect if it weren't for the Indians. But—waugh! It was their country first, he reflected as he drifted into sleep. He would've felt as they did if strangers had come into his land, trapping the beaver, shooting the buffalo and deer.

The wooded hills leveled as the five of them approached the Platte River several days later. A mild west wind was blowing from the eastern slopes of the Rockies, warming the land and melting the snow. Signs of spring were beginning to appear everywhere. Green grass sprouting, frogs and blackbirds calling in the marshes, ducks and cranes flying overhead. As they neared the broad, shallow river, where the ice was already breaking up, they saw many bands of buffalo starting their spring migration.

Hugh and his companions killed several buffalo and then camped along the north bank of the Platte for several days while they made ready for the next step of the journey. The easiest way to get to Fort Atkinson, they decided, was to travel the rest of the way by water—on the Platte and the Missouri. They would make a bullboat to take them downstream.

Marsh and More set to work skinning the buffalo and scraping the hides while Hugh and the others fashioned a framework for the boat from springy willow branches, already turning yellow-green in the spring weather. These they bound together with sinews of the slain buffalo.

When the frame was finished, the men stretched the fresh

hides over the willow branches, stitched them together with sinews, and waterproofed the seams with glue made by adding a little water to ground-up buffalo bones and hoofs and boiling them over a slow fire. Finished in two days, the bullboat resembled nothing more than a giant saucer, about nine feet in diameter. Difficult to steer, it had the advantage of having very little draft—important on a river as shallow as the Platte, which meandered across the marshy plains and was full of sandbars. The Indians often used bullboats, for they were easy to make and could be used where heavier pirogues and other craft could not go.

The next day, after a hearty breakfast of buffalo hump, the five men loaded their gear into the bullboat and set off down the Platte, using flat oars shaped with their axes from cottonwood to steer the prowless boat and help them on their way. The paddles were also handy for pushing off drifting rafts of ice and the occasional bloated carcass of a buffalo drowned in an attempted crossing of the river. As always, they kept a sharp lookout for Indians, who could be on the move in this spring weather.

The shriveled brown grasses of winter were sending up fresh green shoots everywhere, and on either bank of the river were many herds of buffalo, all of them wandering toward the prairies as they grazed. Overhead, formations of geese and other waterfowl flew, heading to their nesting ground farther north.

In early afternoon of the second day in the bullboat, they came to a bend in the meandering river where another river joined it—the Laramie, Hugh thought. This was Pawnee country, and he had lived with them in this territory, hunted with them, and learned their language and customs.

American bison, or buffalo. A mainstay of the Plains Indians for meat and hides, buffalo roamed the western plains in uncounted millions in the early nineteenth century. By the 1880s, however, white settlers and hide hunters had wiped out the huge herds and the species was almost extinct.

The Pawnees were bloodthirsty if they were enemies, as he knew from experience, but he was a blood brother to Chief Black Elk. These Indians, he was confident, would welcome him if they ran into each other. Not like their close relatives, the Arikaras, who'd like to kill every white person they met. Strange, for the Arikaras were very much like the Pawnees and spoke practically the same language.

The river made a wide sweeping bend as they approached the place where the Laramie joined it, the banks lined with willows and cottonwoods, the buds swelling and ready to burst. Paddling around the bend, they saw a cluster of tepees on the north bank. Thirty or forty lodges at least. Children were playing and splashing in the shallow water, and some boys were watching a herd of horses on the near shore. Women were working in front of their lodges, scraping the fat from buffalo hides.

Hugh and the others clutched their rifles as they saw several men appear, alerted by the women and children shouting news of the approaching boat. This looked like a Pawnee village, Hugh told himself. It almost had to be. He just hoped that he was right, for it was too late to try to avoid the Indians.

He held up his hand in peace and shouted a greeting in the Pawnee language. Much to his relief, the nearest warrior on the bank returned the greeting and invited them ashore.

14

Elk Tongue's Treachery

Hugh heaved a sigh of relief. These were Pawnees—friendly Indians. Any Pawnee band would honor his blood tie. Assuring his companions that all was well, he steered the boat toward the bank where the Indians were clustered.

Grounding the bullboat in the sand, Hugh stepped out and climbed ashore. At this closer range he recognized the warrior who had greeted him as Dancing Bear, whom he had last seen when he himself was a Pawnee—one of Black Elk's band. Dancing Bear was a short, thickset Indian, with wrinkled, coppery skin and two long braids of gleaming black hair. He had piercing brown eyes and a large nose framed by flaring ears. As befitted an eminent warrior, he wore several eagle feathers in his hair. Naked to the waist, he was clothed in greasy buckskin breeches and moccasins. As Hugh walked toward him, Dancing Bear's broad face widened into a huge grin, showing a ragged row of stained teeth, with a wide gap where one was missing.

"Red Paint, my brother!" he exclaimed in the Pawnee dialect. "Welcome, you and your friends." He raised his hand once again in greeting, and Hugh returned the salute. Red Paint was the name the Pawnees had given him because he had offered the sack of vermilion to Chief Black Elk when he was about to be burned at the stake. Dancing Bear had been one of the warriors present on that memorable day.

The Pawnee walked up to Hugh and shook hands with him, white-man fashion, then invited Hugh and his friends to come to his lodge for food and talk. Hugh looked back at his four companions, who were waiting in the skin boat, their rifles in hand.

"It's all right," he assured them. "Dancing Bear here is a friend of mine from the old days when I was a Pawnee. He's invited us to his lodge. One of ye—Dutton mebbe?—better stay with the boat, though, to look out fer our rifles and gear. There's a heap of Indians in this camp, and there's bound to be some of 'em that can't resist helpin' themselves to anythin' they find unguarded. As fer the rest of ye—come on!"

Leaving Dutton to guard the rifles and gear, Marsh, More, and Chapman followed Hugh and Dancing Bear as they made their way into the village. Women and children stared at them curiously as they passed, and many dogs circled close, sniffing at their fringed leggings. Hugh greeted several men and women whom he recognized, but he soon realized that this wasn't Black Elk's band. The Indians were great ones, though, for visiting their kin in other villages and getting together from time to time for ceremonies and powwows.

Near the center of the camp they were met by a party of seven warriors, led by one very tall Indian whose dress indicated that he was an important chief. He wore a checkered red-and-blue shirt, fringed doeskin breeches, and moccasins intricately decorated with colored beads. A necklace of grizzly bear claws encircled his neck, and stiff eagle feathers stuck out of his braided hair on either side, like horns. Perched between the feathers, on the crown of his head, was a black stovepipe hat—a hat that Hugh suspected had been lifted from some luckless white victim before he'd been scalped.

The chief fixed glittering black eyes on Hugh, then lifted his hand in formal greeting to the four mountain men and introduced himself as Elk Tongue. They would come to his lodge, he told them, and smoke and eat there. It was a bigger lodge than Dancing Bear's, he explained, glancing briefly at Hugh's old friend—a better place for the Pawnee warriors to meet their pale-faced guests.

Hugh looked at Dancing Bear for his reaction, and the other bowed his head slightly—evidently in silent agreement. His action seemed to indicate that they had better do as Elk Tongue suggested. Dancing Bear's expression was very solemn, Hugh noticed—almost grim. He had a momentary feeling of doubt. Was Dancing Bear trying to tell him something without actually saying it? Well, he'd be on his guard against any suspicious actions, but what could he or his three companions do without their weapons? They had to accept Elk Tongue's invitation.

Without further discussion, they all followed the chief and his party to a big tepee set off from the others on a little knoll. Beckoning for Hugh to follow, Elk Tongue entered the lodge.

Stooping to duck through the flapped opening, Hugh and his companions followed. After them came Dancing Bear and the six warriors who had accompanied Elk Tongue, as well as several others. All of them sat down cross-legged around the central fire pit and waited in silence while Elk Tongue stuffed tobacco into a long pipe and lit it. After waving it in the traditional ceremonial fashion, he took a puff and passed it on to Hugh, who sat next to him. After drawing on the pipe, Hugh in turn handed it to Marsh. Soon it had made the rounds of all the men in the circle.

The dim interior of the tepee was warm and smelled of many different odors—meat bubbling in a pot over the fire, wood smoke, hides, human sweat, leather, and dried herbs. An ancient crone stirred the meat in the pot, and a younger woman placed bark slabs in front of the assembled men. Hugh was hungry and sniffed appreciatively as the thick stew bubbled. He saw the women moving about him, saw several children behind them, watching wide-eyed. The warmth, the anticipation of a full hot meal coming up lulled him into a sense of security and well-being.

A small movement roused him. One of the women was shooing the children from the lodge. He heard the younger woman say something to the older one. The word, he suddenly realized, was not said in the way the Pawnees pronounced it. It was Arikara talk. The speech of the two tribes was almost identical, except for certain words which the Arikaras pronounced with a distinctive accent.

"These are Rees," he muttered in a low tone to Marsh and the other two companions sitting beside him, "not Pawnees. We've been hoodwinked!"

"No Arikaras, we," protested Elk Tongue, who had overheard Hugh's warning. "We Pawnees."

"Come! Let's get out of here!" Hugh exclaimed to the others. Rising suddenly, he dashed out of the lodge, followed closely by Marsh, Chapman, and More. Running as fast as they could, the four mountain men headed back toward the bullboat on the beach, where Dutton waited. Scrambling out of the lodge, Elk Tongue and his men followed in close pursuit.

As they neared the beach, Hugh shouted to Dutton to shove off. He and the others would board the bullboat in midstream; then, with their rifles, they could hold the Indians off till they reached the far shore. His warning was too late, however. Even as he shouted, he saw three warriors heading for the boat. Two of them scooped up the rifles with yells of triumph, while the third dashed at Dutton, brandishing a hand ax.

Turning, Dutton swung his rifle at the warrior, hitting him on the side of the head with the stock and knocking him to the ground. Running back to the bullboat, he discharged his rifle at one of the other two attackers, wounding him. The other man, clutching the stolen weapons, ran away as Dutton got into the boat and shoved off.

Reaching the river bank, Hugh splashed into the shallow water and made his way toward the bullboat as fast as he could go. Marsh and Chapman were close behind him. As they reached the boat and started to climb in, they heard a despairing scream from shore. Hugh glanced back and saw More falter and fall on the river bank, a hatchet buried in his head, several Arikaras around him.

A horde of Arikaras lined the river bank, brandishing bows and rifles and howling in victory. A few even plunged into the water in pursuit as Hugh, Marsh, and Chapman scrambled aboard the bullboat. Several Indians fired their rifles at the mountain men while others launched a volley of arrows at them. The rifle shot splashed around them, and two arrows lodged in the side of the boat, but Hugh and his companions were not touched as they paddled desperately toward the far bank of the river. A half dozen Rees, or more, were swimming after them, and by now the Indians had also launched several of their own bullboats in pursuit. By the time the mountain men reached the other side, the leading warriors were almost upon them.

Scrambling out of the boat, the four men raced toward a nearby sheltering grove of trees, interspersed with tall rock formations. Several arrows hissed past Hugh and, beside him, Chapman uttered an anguished cry. Half turning, Hugh saw his companion stagger forward, then fall, an arrow in his back. With a cry of victory, a Ree warrior was dashing forward to claim his scalp. A half dozen others were close behind him.

A moment later, Hugh was among the trees, shut off from view of the pursuing Indians. Dutton and Marsh, who had been ahead of him, had disappeared—Hugh didn't know whether they had been cut down or not. Running through the tree trunks as fast as he could go, he reached a ledge of rocks into which he climbed. Behind, he heard the exultant yelps of the Indians as they continued the chase. Crawling into a narrow vertical crack between two massive rock ledges, he lay down and quickly covered himself with dead branches and leaves. It was his only chance, he knew. He couldn't outrun the Indians. Two of his companions—More and Chapman—were already dead. He didn't want to go the same way.

Within minutes the Indians were tramping through the wooded slope below the rock ledge, sometimes so close he could have thrown a pebble and hit them. He heard their excited cries as they searched for him—and the others, if they were still alive. All afternoon he lay in the narrow cleft of rock, scarcely daring to breathe as the Indians roamed back and forth, scouring the area.

A bead of sweat trickled down from his forehead onto his nose, and then a fly lit on his ear. He could feel it as it crept about, and the itch that developed was almost unbearable. He wanted nothing in the world so much as to scratch the offending spot, but somehow he resisted the urge. Any movement could be fatal. He gritted his teeth, tried to think of other things, and endured. He heard two nearby Indians calling to one another as they continued to search for him.

Although his body was motionless, Hugh's mind was racing, going over again and again what had happened, seeking answers. This was a Pawnee camp, or had been—he was sure of it. But the Arikaras were there, too. More of them, it seemed like, than Pawnees. Had Dancing Bear been part of the treachery? Or had his old friend been powerless to warn him, or prevent the attack? He would never know, but he thought Dancing Bear would've helped him if he could. One thing was for sure—all the attacking Indians had been Rees, not Pawnees.

Outside, he heard a distant whoop, and then the sound of rifle shots. Had the Arikaras spotted Dutton and Marsh? Had those two gone under, too, along with More and Chapman? And why . . . why . . . he continued to wonder, had the Arikaras been here in the Pawnee camp?

Suddenly he could almost hear his mind click, as a piece of the puzzle fell into place. Elk Tongue! He must have been the warrior the Mandans had told him about at Fort Tilton. He should have guessed! Elk Tongue must have been the Ree warrior who had taken over Chief Gray Eye's band during the Leavenworth campaign last summer, after a mortar shell had beheaded the old chief and the Arikaras had sued for peace. The Rees had headed north to live near the Mandans after the burning of their own villages, but Elk Tongue and his band had headed south to join up with the Pawnees. Hugh felt almost sick. He should have realized! But even if he had, it would've been too late, because by that time he and his companions had met up with the murdering devil.

As dusk settled, the sounds of search subsided. Darkness came and the moon rose—a waxing crescent. The Indian village across the river finally slept. They'd given up their search, Hugh decided. Until morning at least.

Near midnight, Hugh cautiously crept out of his hiding place. Picking his way carefully, he headed eastward on the south bank of the Platte, guided by the dim light of the moon and stars. He thought of Dutton and Marsh, and wondered whether they had survived. No use looking for them, he told himself. If he stumbled into them in the darkness, they'd like as not shoot him, thinking he was a Ree.

By dawn he was nearly a dozen miles from the Indian village. As the sun rose he crossed the Platte, clinging to a log and paddling with his legs until the water shallowed and he could wade ashore. Keeping to the brush beside the river, he traveled as fast as he could all that day, stopping only briefly near noon to dine on a few roots of wild turnip and onion. Although he had lost his rifle and most of the rest of his belongings, he still had his hunting knife and the flint and steel in his pouch. The fact that he had these gave him a feeling of confidence. He'd get by.

The next day he left the Platte and struck north toward the headwaters of the White River. Dim in the distance, he could see the Black Hills rising into the sky, a few of them still covered with snow. Here, in the prairies, the grass was greening, the buffalo wandering past in their multitudes. The days were warm and sunny, the red-winged blackbirds whistling and swaying on the reeds along the marshes. Mallards courted in the shallow waters, and meadowlarks sang their songs in the flower-studded grassland.

Spring! Good to be alive, Hugh thought. Even though he had no rifle, he found food aplenty along the way—the eggs of waterfowl, prairie roots and bulbs. One day he dined on the tender flesh of a newborn buffalo calf, strangely deserted by its mother.

After eating his fill of this windfall and cutting off several steaks of tender veal to take with him, Hugh headed on. Far to the north he could see the peaks of the Black Hills, their tops still snow-covered, their slopes dark green with cedar and pines. When he reached the White River, he followed it through the Badlands with their fantastic formations of red, brown, yellow, and gray rock. One afternoon he watched a band of pronghorns bounding ahead of him, their white rumps bobbing up and down. May had arrived, and the weather was turning hot.

As Hugh plodded eastward, he was always alert for any sign of Indians. Several times, when dust on the horizon indicated that Indians were on the move, he hid among the thickets of willow and cottonwood in the river bottom. Probably friendly Sioux, but after his recent go-round with the Arikaras, he was in no mood to take any chances.

June was no more than a week away when he came at last to the mouth of the White River and saw, just ahead of him, the familiar palisades of Fort Kiowa.

Once inside the friendly walls, he and Young Cayewa filled each other in on what had happened since they last saw one another. Brazeau related how Charbonneau had returned from the Mandan villages early in the spring, bringing with him the news of the massacre of Langevin and the boatmen at the hands of the Arikaras last fall.

"He tell me you leave the boat just a few minutes before the Rees attack," Young Cayewa went on. "He say you almost killed, too. *Mon Dieu!* Tell me what happen."

Hugh described his part in the events and how the Mandans had saved him from the Rees when he'd stumbled into their village several hours later. "Aie! Them Rees are bad 'uns," he exclaimed. Hugh then told Young Cayewa

Bluffs of the Upper Missouri, as seen by Karl Bodmer. The trading post in the distance is Fort Pierre, built at the confluence of the Missouri and Teton, or Bad, rivers. Sioux Indian tepees surround the fort.

about his winter journey to Henry's post on the Little Bighorn, and his recent run-in with Elk Tongue and his band of Rees on the Platte, just a few days ago.

When Brazeau told Hugh that he was sending a mackinaw downriver in several days with a load of furs, as well as letters for Fort Atkinson, Hugh asked if he could go along. He wanted that meeting with John Fitzgerald as soon as possible.

15
Fort Atkinson

Far ahead, Hugh could see the high sandy cliffs of Council Bluffs looming over the western bank of the Missouri, with the stout walls of Fort Atkinson rising from the broad tableland above them. The Missouri River was high with the spring runoff, the waters swift and mud-yellow. Although the distance by river from Fort Kiowa to Fort Atkinson was more than two hundred miles, the mackinaw, aided by the swift current, had made it in just a little more than three days. Hugh had almost reached his goal—the final reckoning with John Fitzgerald. He patted the stock of the rifle that he'd gotten from Young Cayewa.

A few minutes later, he stepped ashore at the big dock near the south end of the bluffs and started up the road leading to the main gate of the fort high above him. It was a busy morning scene. On either side, hordes of workmen were scurrying about, unloading the cargoes of several boats. Wagons filled with all sorts of supplies creaked by, both coming and going. Sweating teamsters shouted at their slow-moving mules and cracked whips over them, urging them on their way.

Halfway up the hill, on the side toward the river, Hugh passed a big commissary store and warehouse. On the other side of the road was a brick building that evidently housed the laundry facilities for the fort. Taking advantage of the warm spring sunshine, a half dozen laundresses were working outside: scrubbing clothes in steaming tubs, rinsing, wringing, hanging the clean laundry on lines to dry. Hugh glanced down at his own ragged and dusty outfit with a wry smile, then shrugged his shoulders and hurried on.

Near the top of the hill he passed a platoon of soldiers heading down to the docks. He stopped in front of a busy blacksmith shop and watched while a dripping smithie pumped his bellows until the fire in his forge was red hot. Then, seizing his tongs, the blacksmith thrust a horseshoe into the fiery mass until it glowed like the noonday sun—ready to be hammered into the desired shape. A horse stood beside him, waiting patiently to be shod. Hugh breathed in the distinctive smell of burning charcoal and hoof parings, the scent of hot leather. His nose crinkled as another wagon creaked past him, this one filled with fresh horse manure.

Too much going on around here, he told himself as he

headed on. Too many people, too danged much civilization. The sooner he finished his business here and headed back to wild country, the better. First, deliver those dispatches he had for General Ashley—and then track down Fitz.

Reaching the top of the trail, he came to the big main gate on the south side of the fort. There, a young downy-faced guard eyed him suspiciously, barring the way with his rifle until Hugh identified himself. The soldier carefully examined the identification papers Major Henry had given Hugh. Finally satisfied, the young man waved him on, pointing out the regimental headquarters at the far end of the parade ground.

"Playin' at bein' a real soldier," Hugh muttered to himself as he passed through the gate. He was fuming with impatience. "Give a farm lad a rifle 'n' a uniform an' he thinks he's a gen'ral!" On he went, past a long barracks for enlisted men, then a row of brick living quarters for officers and their families. He saw a bed of larkspurs and daisies in front of one of the quarters, red geraniums in front of another. Women! he thought. Always wanting to prettify any place they live. In spite of himself, Hugh smiled as he gazed at the blossoms. Ah, well—little enough of beauty they'd see here. The fort was a man's world, and the ladies couldn't get out to see the unspoiled mountains and hills, the wild free birds and the game that were the real glory of this country.

A top sergeant was drilling a company of blue-clad enlisted men in the dusty parade grounds, and Hugh stopped for a moment to watch the precision close-order marching and listen to the shouted commands, the slam of rifle stocks on the hard-packed parade ground. "Hope those boys look as pert when they're facin' a bunch of Indians bent on liftin' their scalps," he observed to himself as he headed on.

At the Sixth Regiment headquarters, close to the high stockade at the north end of the fort, he again submitted to questions and scrutiny before he was finally admitted to the central office where the officer of the day, a captain, was busy writing in a large journal.

"A man here to see you from the Rocky Mountain Fur Company post on the Yellowstone, Captain Riley, sir," the orderly announced. "He has some dispatches fer Colonel Leavenworth 'n' others to be sent on to Gen'ral Ashley in St. Louis. Says he won't give 'em to anyone 'ceptin' Colonel Leavenworth or the officer in charge." The orderly, a corporal, gave all this information with a barely suppressed sneer. Hugh felt his face redden. Conceited little peacock!

Captain Riley looked up. His face was bathed in sweat and he looked tired and harassed. "That will be all," he told the orderly crisply. Rising from his chair, he extended his hand to Hugh and introduced himself. "Bennett Riley," he said. "What can I do for you?" He had a short clipped moustache, and his black hair, slightly curly, was in disarray as he mopped his forehead. "This damned heat," he muttered.

Hugh felt a wave of sympathy for the captain, all rigged up in his hot woolen uniform, when any sensible man would dress to fit the weather—that is, if he had any choice in the matter. Captain Riley didn't.

"Hugh Glass," the mountain man said, and explained

his business at the fort. "Had a bit of Indian trouble on the Platte before gettin' here—but here I be at last," he concluded.

Captain Riley's face lit up with interest as he motioned Hugh into a chair beside his desk. "Tell me about it," he suggested.

As Hugh described the encounter on the headwaters of the Platte with Elk Tongue's band of Arikaras, Captain Riley listened attentively, and from time to time he scribbled some notes on a pad of paper. "I saw More and Chapman killed," Hugh told him, "and, as fer Dutton and Marsh, I never saw them again—probably killed as well. I should've suspected some sort of skullduggery soon as I went ashore, but that sight of my old Pawnee friend, Dancing Bear, put me off completely." He shook his head and sighed. "Should've known better," he admitted.

Captain Riley smiled. "Well, I have news for you, my friend," he said. "Dutton and Marsh arrived here two days ago, hail and hearty. They thought you'd been killed! They left just this morning on a boat for St. Louis. Said they'd take in the sights there before heading back to the Yellowstone."

Hugh's scarred and wrinkled face lit up with a grin. So Dutton and Marsh had made it, after all. That eased his mind a bit. He then asked to see Colonel Leavenworth and pass on the dispatches he had.

"The commanding officer isn't here," Captain Riley told him."He left yesterday for a meeting with General Atkinson at Jefferson Barracks. Won't be back until next week. But if it's dispatches you have for him and General Ashley, I'll sign for them and see that they're delivered."

"Guess that'll be fit 'n' proper," Hugh admitted. Reaching inside his dusty jacket, he drew out the sealed dispatches and gave them to the captain. After quickly checking the names on the envelopes, Captain Riley wrote out a receipt for them and gave it to Hugh.

"There's just one more thing, Captain," Hugh said as he tucked the paper into his pocket. "Now that our official business is over, I'll tell ye I've got some personal business of my own to take care of. I come all this way to find one man—John Fitzgerald. I understand he came here and joined up with the army some time ago."

"John Fitzgerald?" Captain Riley asked. "That name sounds familiar. Let me see. . . ." He drew out a ledger from one of the desk drawers—evidently a roster of the Sixth Regiment personnel. He turned the pages one by one, scanning the names. "Fitzgerald? Yes, here he is. John Fitzgerald. Joined up last April 19." He read the further notation beside the name. "Hmm. He came downriver from Fort Kiowa, said he'd come from Major Henry's fort on the Yellowstone. Well—an old friend of yours?"

"Some might say that," Hugh responded, "but I wouldn't. Still, I have a pretty strong hankerin' to meet up with 'im again."

Something in Hugh's tone made the captain look at him sharply. After a moment of silence, he asked, "And what might you be wanting to see him for?"

"I aim to shoot the skunk, that's why I want to see him."

16
The Final Reckoning

Captain Riley blinked, his face indicating his surprise. He gazed at Hugh Glass for a long moment. "Oh no, you won't," he finally stated, his voice calm but determined. "There'll be no shootin' of any soldier here!" Hitching his chair around so that he faced Hugh directly, he crossed his right leg over his left knee and leaned back. "Now, suppose you tell me what this is all about."

Hugh told him the whole story of Jim Bridger and John Fitzgerald's treachery—how they'd abandoned him, taken all his gear, and left him for dead.

"But I didn't die!" he ended by saying. "I hunkered my

way to Brazeau's post, with nary a rifle, knife, or any fixin's. And from there I set out to track down those two and deal them the same as they gave me."

"And what about the other one?" Riley demanded. "Did you find him at Henry's post on the Yellowstone?"

"The other?" Hugh felt slightly uncomfortable. "Yes, I had it out with that young 'un. He's just a lad and weren't t' blame as much as Fitz. I let him go."

"But you still blame Fitzgerald—is that it?" Captain Riley persisted. "You want to take out your feelings on him?"

"He left me for dead!" Hugh declared fiercely. "He stole my favorite rifle."

"Can't say's I blame you for feeling the way you do," Captain Riley responded. "But there'll be no shootin'! I'll bring him here to face you, though, if you give me your word about that. And if he still has your rifle, I'll see that you get it back. Agreed?"

Hugh nodded reluctantly. "I'll do no shootin' inside the fort," he said.

Captain Riley paused, understanding the significance of Hugh's words. Then he shrugged his shoulders. "Just leave that rifle of yours with me," he said. "I'll hold it for you while you talk to Fitzgerald." He pointed to a door on the opposite side of the room. "Go set yourself in there," he said, "and I'll bring Fitzgerald to you when we locate him." He called for the orderly as Hugh walked over to the door and opened it.

Hugh glanced at the small, bare room. Sparsely furnished with three chairs and a small desk, it was evidently used for private conferences. A portrait of George Washington hung on the wall above the desk. Gazing at it, Hugh felt vaguely uncomfortable. What would that great leader have done in his place? He'd do what had to be done! he muttered fiercely to himself. Washington was a fair man, a just man, determined and fearless. He'd give no quarter to his enemies! An eye for an eye, a tooth for a tooth—that would be his advice.

But even as he said this to himself, he felt a twinge of doubt. Fearless in battle George Washington had been, but he'd also been generous to the enemy, once he'd licked them. Hugh tried to thrust the thought away, but it persisted. Then the image of his Quaker grandmother flashed through his mind. She'd countenance no fighting around her, he reflected. But she'd never had to deal with Indians, or the likes of those who'd leave a body to die in the wilderness. Fitz deserved whatever he, Hugh Glass, would deal out to him, Hugh told himself grimly.

He waited impatiently, squirming and fuming as his mind churned with many conflicting thoughts. A full half hour went by before he heard footsteps outside, saw the door open. In came Captain Riley, John Fitzgerald behind him.

Hugh stood up, a scowl on his face as he stared at Fitz. The man was all decked out in a clean blue uniform, Hugh noted, and his dark hair was cut and freshly slicked back. His face was calm, but his eyes were wary. Drops of perspiration rolled down his forehead, and Hugh could see that he was nervous. In his hands he held Hugh's rifle, Old Faithful. Up to now Fitzgerald had hardly dared to look at him, Hugh noted with grim satisfaction. But finally their eyes met.

"Hello, Hugh," Fitzgerald said, after a moment's hesitation. He took a step toward him and held out the rifle. "Here's yer rifle. I've took good care of it—after that time we left ye fer dead."

"Left me fer dead, did ye?" Hugh thundered. "You two robbed me and abandoned me, then lit out fer safety! All ye cared about was yer own hide!"

"We thought you was dead," Fitzgerald said stubbornly, his face flushing, "or next thing to it! We did our best fer you for five days, Hugh, but when Indian signs showed, we had to leave. You'd be dead any minute, we figgered, an' we knowed you wouldn't want t'pull us under, too. Would you?" He managed a weak smile.

"You abandoned me!" Hugh growled again. "Robbed me and left. I wouldn't treat a dog thataway!" As he said it, he suddenly remembered the old hound dog that gunsmith Wolfson had abused in Pittsburgh. Many a time Hugh had stood between it and the gunsmith's kicks. That dog had worshipped Hugh, and yet he'd left it behind when he took off. Why? He'd always remember its mournful whine as he left. He sighed and was silent.

Captain Riley was eyeing him keenly. "Few men can say they've always done the right thing by everyone every time," he observed. "Can you say that, Hugh?"

"I never done what Fitz done," Hugh declared hotly. "I never turned my back on any man, woman, or child—or any *compañero* of mine that needed help. I never left anyone t'die like this bucko did to me. He jest . . ."

"Hold it, Glass!" Captain Riley interrupted. "Private Fitzgerald says that he and young Bridger did their best for you for five days, and that they left only when they were sure you'd reached the end of your tether and their own lives were on the line. That right?"

For a moment Hugh said nothing. Then he glared scornfully at Fitzgerald. "Seein's how the Army don't allow me t'shoot ye like ye deserve," he added, "just hand over me Old Faithful rifle, John, and be damned to ye. It's you and yer conscience—iffen ye got one—that's gotta live with what ye done."

"You got it all twisted," Fitzgerald declared abruptly, as he handed the rifle back to Hugh. "We done our best fer ye, Hugh—I tell you—you gotta believe me. Iffen we'd stayed, all three of us would a' gone under."

Hugh grunted his disbelief, then turned his back on Fitzgerald and shook Captain Riley's hand. "Thank ye, Captain, fer tryin' t'sort this matter out," he said. "At least I got me rifle back. Guess I'll be on my way." He turned and gazed straight at Fitz. "As fer you," he declared, "stay out'n my way in the future, or I'll blast ye with Old Faithful—soldier or no soldier."

The two men gazed silently after him as he opened the door and headed for the wagon road.

Hugh felt no satisfaction as he walked down toward the docks. He'd met Fitz face to face, as he wanted, and told him what for! Waugh! There wasn't much satisfaction in that! The varmint was still strutting about, safe in his soldier's outfit, slick as a peeled onion!

He felt the resentment festering within him. Nothing he could do about it for the moment, he reminded himself. When he reached the docks, he gazed moodily out over the muddy, swiftly flowing waters of the Missouri, high with the spring snow melt. He cursed silently. Fitz had had it coming to him, but he'd wriggled out of it by becoming a soldier boy. Kicking the dirt beneath his foot in frustration, he turned away from the river. Time to be heading on, he told himself. He'd be on his way first thing in the morning.

That evening, he joined the crew of a keelboat fresh in from St. Louis and ate his evening meal with them. From Hugh's appearance they had quickly spotted him as an old hand and, around the campfire, peppered him with eager questions about what to expect on the Upper Missouri. Was the trapping good? How about the Indians?

Tired and grumpy, Hugh stayed with them until dark, then retired by himself to a grove of cottonwoods that lined a little stream feeding into the big river. Curling up in his blanket, he tried to sleep, but found that he couldn't. Too many restless thoughts were churning about in his mind, too much frustration and too many angry feelings. He tossed restlessly as a stream of images flashed before him: the giant grizzly on top of him, the shock and agony, the long crawl, the hunger, the tramp through the winter snows to reach Fort Henry. Then the confrontation with young Jim and the meeting with Fitz today. Sick at heart, he pounded his fist into the earth. Finally he fell into a troubled sleep, but the images kept coming, this time in the form of dreams.

The image of a slim Indian girl passed before him. She came toward him, smiling, carrying a bowl of steaming buffalo stew. She sat beside him as he ate. Dove—Dove, the Pawnee wife he'd taken when he lived with the Indians. She was Chief Black Elk's daughter—and a dutiful, loving wife she'd been. Yet when the time came, he'd left her—abandoned her, hadn't he? Oh, he'd persuaded himself that she'd never have fit into the white man's world. She'd be far happier staying with her father's tribe. He'd told himself that he'd return sometime—but he never had!

He woke, beads of sweat on his forehead. Yes—he'd abandoned her! Just as Jim and Fitz had abandoned him. He was as bad as they were—worse, maybe. He groaned, trying to clear his mind of all thoughts. He got up, unable to sleep any more that night, and went down to the shore of the big river. Hunched up on the bank, he gazed out over the dark waters. Above, countless stars glittered in the clear sky.

What was right? he wondered. What was the right thing for a man to do in any particular situation? The image of Chapman falling beside him with an Arikara arrow in his back flashed into his mind. Could he have saved him if he'd tried? No—common sense told him that he'd have been dead, too, if he'd stopped, even for a moment, with that bunch of Arikaras coming on.

The red sun was just rising above the bluffs on the opposite shore when Hugh finally stood up. Time to gather his gear and be on his way, he told himself. He walked over to the road leading to the docks. The sun was climbing steadily above the distant shore, and already men were stirring in the boats and starting to head down from the fort on the high bluffs. One man in particular came toward him. An unarmed soldier. John Fitzgerald.

Fitz walked straight up to Hugh, then stopped and looked him in the eye. "Hoped I'd find you before you headed off," he said. "I couldn't leave it the way you did yesterday! You got it wrong, Hugh!"

"Do I?" Hugh grunted. In spite of himself, he felt a surge

of sympathy as he faced the other man. It had taken some spirit for Fitz to come down here unarmed, looking for him. "Ain't we said all there is to be said?" he finally demanded.

"No, we ain't, Hugh!" Fitzgerald responded with emotion. "Yesterday you tried to strip me of every bit of pride I ever had, and if a man ain't got pride, he ain't got nuthin'. I ain't as bad as you tried to make out, Hugh," he went on. "Go ahead and shoot me if ye must, but I'm tellin' you again we did our best fer ye all those five days we stayed with ye. We left only when it was a question of all three of us dyin' if we'd stayed."

"I hear ye, Fitz," Hugh responded, "and I guess you really believe it. Fact remains—the two of ye left me to die. I wouldn't a' done that!"

"Well, I see it different," Fitzgerald said. "You think we should've stayed, but my bet is that if we had, all three of us would've been dead by now. As it is, we're all alive an' kickin'. What's wrong with that?"

Hugh pondered Fitzgerald's words for several minutes. He could see that Fitz really believed that he and young Bridger had done the right thing when they'd left him. Well—maybe so. It all depended on the point of view.

"All right, Fitz," he said after a lengthy silence, "what's done is done, an' from the way you look at it, mebbe you're right. You're what you be, and I'm what I be. It's yerself you've gotta live with, and in the future, I trust you'll do yer best for yer soldier *compañeros* when ye get in a tight squeeze."

As he said the words, Hugh felt a tremendous lightening of his spirits. He'd done the right thing, he reckoned. Now,

Buffalo drinking water and bathing at night on the Platte River. Watercolor by Alfred Jacob Miller.

don't let the past fester anymore. Just look to the future.

"Guess I'll be on my way," he said, picking up Old Faithful and his blanket roll. "Good luck to ye," he forced himself to add, nodding curtly to Fitzgerald. Turning his back on him, he started walking back toward the docks. For a long moment, Fitzgerald gazed after him. Then he started up the road to the fort.

Once again Hugh gazed out over the wide Missouri, watching as the strong current swept uprooted trees and other debris past him. Overhead a flock of ducks flew past. At last he went back to the road south of the fort and headed toward the broad, green prairies to the west, wildflowers blooming in them now. He sniffed the air. Cleaner, clearer here than in the fort.

On beyond were the mountains. Mountains and wild rivers. Buffalo and beaver. Yes—Indians and grizzly bears, too—and the fewer whites the better. He'd head on out again. He'd hunt and trap and live in God's free and glorious country. That's where he belonged.

Afterword

After the turbulent adventures which Hugh Glass lived through in 1823 and 1824, recorded history provides only a few more scraps of information about his subsequent life and activities.

A year or so after his rendezvous with John Fitzgerald at Fort Atkinson, Hugh's old friend George Yount related that Hugh was in Taos, New Mexico. He had gone there, he said, to guide a band of trappers into the territory of the Utes. Heading north and west from Taos, the party eventually reached an area some seven hundred miles distant—perhaps the Snake River area of Idaho or Oregon.

Traveling from one camp to another by canoe, the party harvested many beaver pelts.

One day they sighted a solitary Indian woman—probably a Shoshone—digging for roots on the river bank. The trappers decided to give her several beaver carcasses which they had just skinned, for the Indians considered beaver meat, especially the tail, a delicacy. Paddling their pirogue ashore, Hugh Glass and another trapper got out, each carrying a beaver carcass for the woman.

The woman was unaware of their approach, and when she finally turned and saw them, she took off with a startled scream. Alerted by her cries, nearby warriors hastened to her defense and let fly a shower of arrows at the trappers. Glass's companion fell, mortally wounded. Glass turned back to try to save his friend, but quickly realized that the man was dying. Urging Hugh to save himself, his stricken companion asked only that Hugh recharge his rifle so that he might have one more shot at the Indians before he died. This Hugh did, then headed back toward the waiting canoe as fast as he could go. As he reached it, an arrow buried itself deep in his back.

Except for the one mortally wounded trapper, the party escaped; and Hugh carried that arrow, lodged close to his spine, for seven hundred miles, until they returned to Taos. There, a hardy volunteer doctor gave Hugh a beaker of whiskey to dull his pain, and a bullet to bite, and with his razor cut out the deeply embedded arrowhead from the festering wound. Hugh bore the operation with hardly a grunt of pain and quickly recovered from the ordeal.

In 1828 Hugh was trapping in the far Northwest, possibly in the Yellowstone region. There, as Kenneth Mc-

Bighorn sheep on high bluffs of the Upper Missouri, from a painting by Karl Bodmer.

Kenzie, director of the powerful American Fur Company, records, the free trappers not associated with any fur company sent Hugh Glass as their agent to bargain with him on their behalf. The American Fur Company was then trying to dominate and take over the entire fur trade in the western territories. The company's headquarters was at Fort Union, built near the old Fort Henry at the mouth of the Yellowstone. Glass met with McKenzie at the fort and carried his proposals back to the trappers who had shown their trust and faith in Hugh by sending him to parley with the American Fur Company in the first place.

What happened to the two men—John Fitzgerald and Jim Bridger—who had abandoned Hugh Glass at the forks of the Grand, and whom Hugh had subsequently tracked down, confronted, and forgiven?

John Fitzgerald, a private in the U.S. Army at Fort Atkinson, served a five-year hitch with the Sixth Regiment, his occupation listed as carpenter. In 1825 he was one of the soldiers who accompanied the Atkinson-O'Fallon expedition up the Missouri to the Yellowstone region. On April 19, 1829, his term of enlistment having expired, he was given an honorable discharge at Jefferson Barracks, Missouri. What happened to him after that we don't know.

Jim Bridger, the young and inexperienced mountain man of 1823, went on to become one of the most famous and respected of that strange breed of men who faced the western wilderness as beaver trappers and explorers. He was one of those who helped discover the South Pass, the gateway through the Rockies. In the winter of 1824–25, he was the first white man to visit the Great Salt Lake. In 1830 he became one of the partners of the Rocky Mountain Fur Company; later he was in the service of the American Fur Company.

In 1843 Bridger built a fort and trading post on the Black's Fork of the Green River in the southwest corner of present-day Wyoming—a post which served travelers on the Oregon Trail for many years. As time went on, he also worked for the government as a guide through the western wilderness and became preeminent in this occupation.

Throughout his long life, as stated by Stanley Vestal, one of his biographers, "Jim Bridger looked out for other men until his nickname—'Old Gabe'—became a synonym for courage, unselfishness, generosity, looking out for others less capable or more reckless than himself. Sometimes a bad mistake in early life proves to be the making of a man—if he has the makings of a man. . . ."

Hugh Glass, who lived through so many exciting adventures and had so many hairbreadth escapes, seemed to bear a charmed life. The Arikara Indians, however, the tribe he had met with and fought with and escaped from so many times, finally proved his nemesis.

In the winter of 1832–33, Hugh was at Fort Cass, an American Fur Company post on the Yellowstone River, several miles south of the mouth of the Bighorn. This was in the country of the friendly Crow Indians, and no one would expect any wandering Arikara warriors to be in the vicinity—especially in midwinter. But some were there.

"Old Glass, with two companions, had gone from Fort Cass to hunt beavers on the Yellow Stone," recounts George Yount, "and as they were crossing the river on the ice farther down, they were all three shot, scalped and plundered by a war party of thirty Arikaras, who were concealed on the opposite bank."

"When Hugh was buried in an unfound grave beside the Yellowstone," writes his biographer John Myers Myers, "pristine wilderness and an unlimited fur market were still viewed as changeless verities. . . . Glass functioned when and where settlement wasn't yet dreamed of, and he had no more use for a tie to any piece of real estate than he had for the leg-irons of organized society."

For an epitaph, his fellow mountain man George Yount may have said it best: "All must admit that there was in this brawny trapper a fortitude & a capacity for endurance such as rarely falls to the lot of mortal man—And such a series of adventures, dangers & sufferings has rarely fallen to the lot of humanity—

"He had his failings," Yount admitted. "—But his fellow

On a rise a half mile south of the forks of the Grand River and about ten miles south of Lemmon, South Dakota, a marker dedicated to the memory of Hugh Glass was erected in 1964 by the Lemmon Chamber of Commerce, the State Historical Society, and the Game, Fish and Parks Commission.

trappers bear testimony to his honor, integrity & fidelity—He could be relied on—& no man would fly more swiftly, nor contribute more freely to the relief of a suffering fellow man than he—"

Artists on the Far Western Frontier

In the 1830s, just a few years after the adventures of Hugh Glass as related in this book, three very gifted, pioneering artists—George Catlin, Karl Bodmer, and Alfred Jacob Miller—made their way to the West. There, these three recorded in drawings and paintings the Plains Indians, the mountain men, and the wild, free life of the western wilderness with more immediacy and vivid detail than had ever been done.

GEORGE CATLIN (1796–1872), the first on the western scene, grew up in central Pennsylvania. Self-taught as an artist, he went to St. Louis in 1830, determined to record the life of the Indians and portray primitive man "in the simplicity and loftiness of his nature." In 1832, only a few months before the death of Hugh Glass, Catlin ascended the Missouri River to the mouth of the Yellowstone, sketching and painting the Mandans and other Indian tribes along the way. During the next four years he traveled extensively through the Southwest, in the Rockies, and up the Mississippi River to its source, recording the life and activities of native Americans wherever he went. These drawings and paintings remain his enduring monument.

KARL BODMER (1809–1893), a Swiss by birth, received his art training in Paris. In 1832 he was hired by Prince Maximilian of Wied-Neuwied, an eminent German explorer and scientist, to accompany him to America to "illustrate a scientific safari into the Far West." In 1833 they ascended the Missouri River to Fort Union, and then to Fort Mackenzie on the Marias River. During this extended journey, Bodmer painted many beautiful and detailed watercolors of Indian activities and Missouri River scenes. After returning to Europe in 1834, he worked with skilled engravers to make plates from his watercolors to illustrate Maximilian's book, *Travels in the Interior of North America.* The meticulous draftsmanship and detail of his work have been acclaimed ever since.

ALFRED JACOB MILLER (1810–1874), the son of a Baltimore grocer, studied portraiture in Philadelphia and classical and historical painting in Paris. Returning to America, he made his living as a traveling portrait artist. In 1837 he was invited by Scotsman William Drummond

Stewart to accompany him on a hunting trip along the Platte River and the route of the future Oregon Trail. Miller was to make sketches of what he saw, and later render them into large oil paintings for Stewart's castle in Scotland. The oil paintings that resulted were undistinguished, but Miller's quickly sketched, on-the-spot watercolors of Indians and western scenes bring the past to vivid life. Art critic James Thomas Flexner notes that they "make us feel, with heightened pleasure, that we are actually there."

Catlin, Bodmer, and Miller continued to paint throughout their lives, but all three are best known for the work they did early in their careers, on the western frontier in the 1830s.

Acknowledgments

Years ago, while pursuing research on another subject, I stumbled upon the saga of Hugh Glass. This story of betrayal, survival, a search for revenge, and ultimate forgiveness fascinated me; I determined to sometime write a book about this rugged individual who was a legendary figure in the annals of the fur trade. In the years since, I have explored many different sources and learned as much as I could about his life and times. I soon found out that the contemporary accounts of Hugh's adventures, although in broad agreement concerning the main events, differed so much in detail that it was impossible to know exactly what had happened to him in each incident. It was because of this that I wrote his story as fiction rather than biography.

I gratefully acknowledge my indebtedness to all those original sources, and to the many authors—especially those noted in my suggestions for further reading—who have written about Glass in the more than one hundred fifty years since those days when he roamed the Missouri River and Yellowstone River basins.

Many librarians, archivists, curators, and other individuals too numerous to list have been very helpful and cooperative during the course of my research on Glass. Particular thanks go to my old friend Earl Chace of Rapid City, South Dakota, who accompanied me on an extended tour through the region where many of Glass's adventures occurred in the Dakotas; to Douglas W. Ellison of Medora, North Dakota, who furnished valuable background material; to William E. Lind, Military Reference Branch of the National Archives, who answered my questions about the military service of John Fitzgerald; to Edward J. Drea, Chief, Staff Support Branch, Military History, Department of the Army; and to Steve Kemper, Superintendent of Fort Atkinson State Historical Park, Nebraska, who sent me detailed information about that historic fort.

I owe a great deal to the interest and help given by librarians and other staff at the Amherst Town Library, the Forbes Library in Northampton, the Robert Frost Library and Mead Art Gallery of Amherst College (all of these in Massachusetts); to librarians and research staff at the various museums of the Smithsonian Institution in Washington, D.C.; and to my good friends Edwards Park,

Anne Kobor, Louise Scott, and Judy Barker, all of whom have helped me in my search for illustrations for the book.

Last, but not least, thanks to my editor, Andrea Curley, for her help and support; and my profound gratitude to my wife, Gale, for her suggestions and constant encouragement during the writing of the manuscript, and for her invaluable help in getting it ready for publication.

For Further Reading

One of the most colorful periods in American history—the era of the American fur trade, mountain men, and the exploration and opening of the West—reached its peak in the 1820s and 1830s and then faded under the relentless march of settlement and civilization. For readers who would like to learn more about this era, and about Hugh Glass, Jim Bridger, and their contemporaries, the following books should be of interest:

Alter, Cecil J. *James Bridger, Trapper, Frontiersman, Scout and Guide: A Historical Narrative.* Norman, Oklahoma: University of Oklahoma Press, 1979. Originally published in 1925 (Salt Lake City, Utah: The Shepard Book Company), this long and detailed biography presents a full account of Bridger's involvement with Hugh Glass and the grizzly bear, and includes several of the early newspaper accounts of the adventure.

Caesar, Gene. *King of the Mountain Men: The Life of Jim Bridger*. New York: E. P. Dutton & Co., 1961. This account of Jim Bridger's life includes an interesting version of his part in the Hugh Glass story.

Camp, Charles L., ed. "The Chronicles of George C. Yount." *California Historical Society Quarterly,* April 1923, Vol. 2, pp. 24–33. Yount, a contemporary and friend of Hugh Glass, related this version of Hugh's life and adventures, many years after their occurrence, to a clergyman named Clark, who, fortunately, wrote it all down.

Chittendon, Hiram M. *The American Fur Trade of the Far West.* 2 volumes. Lincoln, Nebraska: University of Nebraska Press, 1986. This landmark history of the fur trade, first published in 1902 (New York: Francis P. Harper), is must reading for anyone interested in the era of the mountain men and fur trappers. Detailed accounts of the Hugh Glass ordeal appear in Vol. II, Chapter 8.

Cooke, Philip St. George. *Scenes and Adventures in the Army*. Philadelphia: Lindsay & Blakiston, 1857. Chapters 19 and 20 of this work give an interesting account of the Hugh Glass story, as originally printed in the *St. Louis Beacon,* December 2–9, 1830.

Guthrie, A. B., Jr. *The Big Sky*. Boston: Houghton Mifflin Co., 1947. This classic novel of mountain men and the fur trade is available in a Bantam Books reprint, 1984.

Kherdian, David. *Bridger: The Story of a Mountain Man.* New York: Greenwillow Books, 1987. This well-written book for young readers describes many of Bridger's adventures during his first years as a mountain man, but does not include the Hugh Glass story.

Manfred, Frederick. *Lord Grizzly*. New York: McGraw-Hill, 1954. This splendid account of Hugh Glass's adventures, told in fictional form, is available as a Bison paperback, University of Nebraska Press, 1983.

Morgan, Dale L. *Jedediah Smith and the Opening of the West*. Indianapolis: Bobbs-Merrill Company, 1953. This outstanding biography is an authoritative account of the history of the Rocky Mountain Fur Company and all of its members, including Hugh Glass. Reprinted as a Bison paperback, University of Nebraska Press, 1964.

Myers, John Myers. *Pirate, Pawnee and Mountain Man: The Saga of Hugh Glass*. Boston: Little, Brown and Company, 1953. Reprinted by the University of Nebraska Press in 1976 as a Bison paperback. In this interesting book, Myers examines all the conflicting accounts and source materials that contribute to the Hugh Glass legend and, after carefully sifting all the evidence, relates what he believes actually happened.

Neihardt, John G. *The Splendid Wayfaring: The Exploits and Adventures of Jedediah Smith and the Ashley-Henry Men, 1822–1831*. New York: Macmillan, 1920. Reprinted in 1970 by the University of Nebraska Press as a Bison Book. Chapter 10 tells of Hugh Glass reaching Fort Henry on the Yellowstone and of his confrontation with the younger of the two men who had abandoned him on the forks of the Grand.

———. *The Song of Hugh Glass*. New York: Macmillan, 1924. This long narrative poem, one part of a sweeping epic (*A Cycle of the West,* Macmillan, 1949), tells the story of Hugh Glass and Jim Bridger and their mutual ordeals. In 1971 it was reprinted as one section of *The Mountain Men,* a University of Nebraska Press Bison Book.

Vestal, Stanley. *Jim Bridger, Mountain Man*. New York: William Morrow & Company, 1946. A reliable, readable, and interesting account of the life of Bridger, including an account of the Hugh Glass story.